I0598678

# Never Land

## Volume 2 of the Never Knights Series

kailin gow

**Never Land (The Never Knights #2)**

This is a YA-Mature/New Adult novel which may contain scenes not suitable for younger teens. Recommended age of reading is 17 years and up.

**Kailin Gow**

Never Land (The Never Knights #2)
Published by THE EDGE
THE EDGE is an imprint of Sparklesoup Inc.
Copyright © 2012 Kailin Gow

For information, please contact:

THE EDGE at Sparklesoup
14252 Culver Dr., A732
Irvine, CA 92604
www.theEDGEbooks.com
First Edition.
Printed in the United States of America.

ISBN: 978-1-59748059-8

# DEDICATION

For anyone who dare to dream.

# Prologue

London was burning. The sweat on my body and the lights that illuminated the club; the heat emanating from all of us in a single, nuclear force – all of these conspired to make the stage look like it was on fire. Steve's drums were deafening – powerful sticks hitting and throbbing against the center of the set, each clash echoing throughout the room. The guitar licks sent shivers up and down my body; I watched as the dancers moved and swayed and shouted in unison, singing along to our songs. Beautiful people – models, actors, socialites, all falling under our spell. All charmed by our power.

> *"You said that you loved me/but I'm not sure*
> *I've been burned by you before."*

My voice hardly sounded like my own. Eerily echoing out of the microphone, it was louder than I was used to. Stronger. Filled with a magic that seemed to transform it from the voice of a nervous, eighteen-year-old girl into something far greater. A voice that could affect each and every one of these people, a voice that could get inside their heads and hearts and make them dance like their lives depended on it. The sweat was pouring down my body and I could catch a glimpse of sweat, too, on the faces of my bandmates, who were rapt in concentration, lost in the music. And I was lost, too – wandering through a labyrinth of sound, trying to find my way out of this energy, this power, this beautiful music that at once belonged to me and yet was something wholly other, some great mystery I had only just begun to learn how to unfold. The song was catchy – mesmerizing, even – but it was more than that. Its beauty haunted me – now more than ever. I had written the lyrics – they were part of me, etched on my heart.

But the music...

I hadn't written that alone. Some chord changes, some waverings of my voice – those I had come up with on my own. Those seemed familiar to me, even natural. But every now and then I changed key, or switched to a minor chord, or the sound of an A diminished wailed over the amplifiers – and then I remembered. Remembered that I hadn't written this song by myself. That another voice, another mind, was here in the room with me, even though he was so far away...

*Danny...*

My heart ached, even now. But I couldn't let myself think about that. Not when I had to put on a brave face in front of so many thousands – even tens of thousands – of people. Not when I had to convince them that I was more than just Keith Knight's protege daughter. I had to convince them that I was a rock star.

And from the wild sounds of their applause, it sounded like I was succeeding. When the song came to an end my voice was hoarse, husky. But even now it was filled with joy. Being onstage was exhilarating for me, for all of us. Only when I was singing did I truly feel as if I was home. And the audience picked up on that. They knew it as well as I did – that I was where I belonged, right here in the O2 arena, opening for My Bloody Valentine.

Six months ago we could never have dreamed this would happen. Six months ago, I was just starting college at USC, trying to fit in, trying to convince myself I wanted a normal life. But a lot had changed since then.

"Ladies and gentlemen," I began, my voice hardly wavering. "I give you – the Never Knights."

The crowd was riotous with joy. I recognized a few faces – celebrities I'd seen on the covers of British tabloids, aspiring reality stars and minor members of the Royal Family. But most of the crowd was full of strangers. A blessed relief, I thought, after LA – where the club scene was dominated by the same few faces, the same familiar smiles. Here everyone was new – the whole scene was wild, was different. Nobody knew us here; nobody had seen my pictures on TMZ or Gawker. They were willing to accept us on one thing alone: the music.

"I'm Neve Knight, on vocals." The crowd responded almost immediately to me, a writhing mass of applause, of adoration. *You could get drunk on this*, I thought to myself, feeling myself bathed in the glow of their love. I felt dizzy just standing there before them. I was reeling – exhausted. And yet I wouldn't have given this up for anything in the world.

"And this is Steve Saint Clair, on drums..." I remembered how it had been only a few months ago, giving this same speech in a nightclub in Los Angeles. How much younger we had been then. Before the night everything changed. Before I'd met *him*. Shiny new stage name aside, Steve was still the same as ever. Muscular, but gawky, charming, with an indomitably goofy smile that made girls giggle and swoon at the same time. He was the most solid of us – the only one who had come through the latest drama unscathed. Steve had never worried about anything but the band – he was the only one, for all his one-night stands, who never let his relationships come between him and the band. Something I knew I couldn't say for myself.

"And Lucky Luc, on keyboards." The girls went wild as Luc fixed his soulful chocolate-brown stare on the audience. *Lucky Luc, all right...*I thought. Our agent had picked the name – figured that a guy with killer looks like his had the luck of one in a million. But I knew that beneath Luc's movie-star good looks there lay a veneer of darkness, of sadness I was unable to crack. Luc hadn't been as violent as Kyle when he'd found out that Danny and I were dating. He hadn't threatened to leave the band overtly – as Kyle had done. But I'd seen the pain I caused in those deep brown eyes. I'd seen how hard it was for him to agree to stay, knowing that the girl he'd kissed in a moment of weakness, the girl he'd finally admitted his feelings to after so many years keeping it quiet, was in love with someone else. I couldn't talk to him about it, of course. We'd agreed to act like it never happened – to forget that kiss. But I knew that things weren't as they were between us. Whatever Luc felt for me, it hadn't gone away. And when he turned that classic, heart-melting stare upon me, it was getting even harder for me to catch my breath.

"And, on bass guitar, Kyle X." The other boys had changed their names for reasons of fame and fortune – because they wanted to re-invent themselves in the manner of their rock icons, taking on stage names that meant something to them. But in changing his name, I knew, Kyle Jostens was doing more than playing a part. He was running away from something. Running from the father whose name he bore, the father who had shot his mother and was serving twenty to life in a federal penitentiary in California. But then again, Kyle was always running. From the pain – from the terror of abandonment, that had set in the day he lost the only family he'd ever known in a single, fell swoop. For years I'd been Kyle's family, his confidante. Like a sister to him.

But no more. He'd admitted his feelings for me – more than that, he'd let his desire for me get between the band. Threatened to walk out if Danny Blue stayed another day. I'd done what was necessary to make him stay – I'd apologized, cried, bitten down my pride and my anger and admitted I was wrong to fall for Danny Blue, even as my heart still told me I was right.

He'd agreed, in the end, to stay. Slowly, grudgingly. But he'd agreed nonetheless. But on one terrible condition.

"Geoff Galaxy, on guitars." It was hard even to form the words. Once upon a time, Geoff had been a true part of the band, one of our best friends. But for a few years now, drugs and alcohol had worked their way into Geoff's system, making him a mere shadow of the man he was. Geoff was still heart-breakingly beautiful; his shaved head and glinting earring still gave him the appearance of a dissolute pirate. And now that his hand had healed, he played guitar as well as he ever did. But something about him didn't sit right with me. It wasn't just the way he looked at me – smirking, predatory, as if he knew the real reason we invited him back into the band. It was the knowledge that cocaine and – no doubt – heroin had burned away some portion of humanity in his brain; the knowledge that the dangerous, devil-may-care persona he projected onstage was more than just an act.

Geoff was a ticking time bomb, and everybody knew it.

But in the absence of Danny Blue, he was the only chance we had. My heart sank as I remembered how Danny had once stood where Geoff was standing now, his smile genuine, his face unscarred by the ravages of drugs and drink. It had been a month since Danny had graciously stepped down from the band, knowing it was the only way to reconcile me and Kyle. And during that month I hadn't stopped missing him.

My heart skipped a beat as I remembered. *Tonight.* Tonight Danny's semester ended – his TA-ing gig at USC over for the semester. Tonight he was coming to London to celebrate Christmas and New Year's with me. I'd taken the year off to go touring – meaning that both of the obstacles between me and Danny had been removed in one fell swoop. He was no longer my band mate and no longer my TA.

That should have made things easy. Instead, we had an ocean between us. And hadn't seen each other in a month. Until tonight...

"Well done," a gorgeous black woman with long, curly hair and a killer smile approached us. She was Cassandra Curry, the PR machine RRR had appointed for us shortly after signing us to their label. But she looked every inch the rock star. "A great start to your touring season. But the press is going to want photos. Look candid, okay guys?" She looked me up and down. "White leather dress," she assessed my clothing. "Vivienne Westwood?"

I nodded, stunned at the breadth of her knowledge.

"Not a bad choice," she smiled. "Shows off your skin. And the spikey boots are a nice touch, too. Although normally I avoid Cavalli's winter collections." She nodded. "I'll put them both on the label's tab. Fashion's part of marketing, after all."

She led us across a red carpet. The crowd passed over us in a blur – a whirl of screams, applause, autographs, blown kisses – and then we were safely backstage, digging into an enormous cake the venue had provided for us.

### Never Land (The Never Knights #2)

Kyle looked utterly exhausted. His bright blue eyes shone with joy – but I could see the melancholy within. Things hadn't been the same with us since our fight. He'd shown me a side of himself I'd never wanted to see – a crazed, obsessive darkness that I could forgive, but not forget. Kyle did more than love me – he *needed* me. And it was this need, a need I could never fulfill, that made things so terrible between us.

"Congratulations, Neve," he said in a small voice. "We've always dreamed about this, you know. Ever since we were kids. Performing in London. Birthplace of punk rock. And at the O2 arena, no less, opening for My Bloody Valentine..."

"I know!" *We'd made it.* We'd lived the dream. In that moment I wanted so badly for things to go back the way to they used to be, for Kyle and I to be normal with each other again. I couldn't resist it. I let my arms surround him, hugging him tightly, the way I'd done in the old days. *Wishing it could be the way it was in the old days.* I pressed his head to mine. "We did it."

I felt his body tense up. I felt his breathing grow shallow. No sooner did he turn his baby-blue eyes to mine then I knew it had been a mistake. Our faces were close – painfully close. And I knew then that I'd given him hope.

"Neve..." he said hoarsely, his voice ragged with emotion.

I immediately stepped away. "Kyle, I'm so sorry..." I said as quickly as I could. "Was that weird? I didn't mean to be weird..."

I couldn't give him hope. Not now. Not with Danny on his way to Heathrow as we spoke.

"No, I'm sorry..." Kyle looked down. "I've been a jerk, Neve, I know that. I knew that when I signed up for the band again. That you're with Danny now. I get that. I respect it. But that doesn't mean it's not still hard. I can't just turn off my feelings like a tap." He smiled wanly, trying hard to look nonchalant. "But for your sake. For the sake of the band. I have to try."

"I know, Kyle." I tried to give him a "buddy" pat on the shoulder. "We'll keep things professional from now on."

"As if that would help," he muttered under his breath. "I just need time, Neve. That's all. Time to get used to this."

I nodded. "I understand."

Steve interrupted our reverie, turning up with a girl on each arm. *Typical Steve,* I thought. Clearly he wasn't hung up on emotional drama. "These two want to come back to our suite," he smiled. "But I can't give them both the attention they deserve." He looked the girls up and down. "How about I bring along my friend Kyle here!"

Their enthusiastic moans made it clear what they thought of this proposal.

"So, Kyle can join us? Will you, Kyle?"

Kyle looked at me for a second, holding my gaze. I could feel his anguish, and even now it had the power to move me.

"Yeah, sure," Kyle said, moving away and following Steve.

No sooner had he gone than my phone rang. My heart leaped at the name on my caller ID: DANNY BLUE.

"Hello, love." His voice still had the power to galvanize me. "I've graded all the term papers – all twenty-five of them. And you know what that means?"

My body began to tingle.

"I've got nothing to do for the next leg of the flight except think about you. I'm sitting in Dublin airport right now, waiting for my connecting flight. If all goes well, I'll have you in my arms in a few short hours."

"Dublin, already?"

"Good winds," said Danny. "We got in early. Now I suggest you take a nap, love. Because you're not getting any sleep tonight."

His voice made me tremble with desire.

"Goodbye, love," he said.

"Goodbye – love you."

"See you soon."

My heart sank. He still hadn't said it back – those three little words I couldn't *stop* saying. I knew the history of his heart. Knew about the girl he had loved, whom he had accidentally killed – the girl I could never be. *Peyton.*

Had he said *I love you* to her?

I sighed and tried to ignore the prickling feelings of doubt. Danny and I were together, were happy. Why did I have to ruin it with my neuroses?

"So, Neve." A harsh, cold voice made me turn around. "I hear you got loads of action when I was away? I thought you were saving yourself, huh? But I guess you're just a dumb slut like all the rest."

**Never Land (The Never Knights #2)**

My heart sank.

It was Geoff.

# Chapter 1

Geoff's eyes were wild and bloodshot as he turned to me. He'd been drinking, I could tell. But more than that – the look in his eyes clearly spoke of much harder substances. His words were slurred and his expression had a lascivious glint in them that spelled clear danger. My stomach dropped. Clearly his time away from the band – first in physical therapy, then, I'd heard, in a spot of parent-mandated rehab – hadn't done much for him. He was still the same messy addict who'd come onto me in a Los Angeles nightclub. His words stung, but I tried to ignore them. *For the good of the band*, I told myself. We only had to stick with Geoff for a few more performances. Then we could find a more reliable guitarist...

Geoff pushed against me, causing me to trip back against the wall. In that moment I became suddenly, terribly conscious of the fact that he and I were alone. His trembling hands found their way to my thighs, gripping the flesh so hard I yelped.

"Careful, Neve..." Geoff said. "The paps are out there. Don't want to make a scandal for the band, do you?" he groaned. "You look so fucking good, you know. In that little skin-tight leather dress. You know you're asking for it, don't you, in that thing? Because no man can resist doing things to you – you must know that, don't you, baby?"

The smell of whiskey on his mouth frightened me. But more so the look in his eyes. Frenetic – crazed. I knew something was wrong with him. Terribly, terribly wrong. This wasn't just a normal bender. This was something worse – far worse. Whatever Geoff had taken tonight, it had made him uncontrollable, savage.

I had to keep calm. "Geoff," I said, as serenely as I could. "You're a bit drunk. You've taken some pills. What you really want is to back down, okay? To sit down. You don't want to provoke me..." I couldn't resist getting mad as I gave his hands a hard shove when he his hands touched mine. "I *will* let you have it, Geoff. If you don't leave me alone."

"Let me have it, huh?" Geoff drawled, his mouth contorting into a cruel grin. "That sounds so good, doesn't it? Coming out of your sexy, *sexy* mouth. I want you to let me have it all night long, you know what I'm saying? I've fantasized about you so many times in the past few months. You're the number one star. I used to have to just dream about what you looked like naked. But then, now I have visual proof..."

"What are you talking about, Geoff?" I inched towards the door, looking for a clean exit.

"You know your dumb dopehead roomie in the dorms? All it took was a few bags of the finest weed in LA and she let me set up a camera in your rooms. I got a good long look at you." He licked his lips.

My mouth fell open. "You made a sex tape of me?"

"Like you wouldn't do the same," he scoffed. "You and the rest of the band tried to fuck me over. To get rid of me to make way for the sainted Danny Blue. I just wanted protection – just to make sure that you'd never turn your backs on me again..." He laughed.

"You're bluffing."

But Geoff didn't look like he was in much of a state to bluff. "I watched it every night while *healing* from my wounds. Maybe you'd call it obsession. I just call it justice.

And I bet you wouldn't want *that* posted on TMZ for Daddy to see."

My jaw dropped. This was insane – even coming from Geoff.

"No, Geoff – you can't..."

"Sure I can." He pulled out his cell phone. "It's on here – not *just* on here, of course. I made copies. But one click of the button and it's leaked to every single gossip site out there."

"Geoff, you can't be serious."

"Probably good for the band. You'd sell more records. Of course, you'd also get sick weirdos like me jacking off to you naked – but that's not my problem, is it?" he laughed.

"Geoff, please...."

"Begging, are we?" He looked amused. "You don't have to beg. You can have this tape back anytime you want. You know what you have to do..."

"What?" My heart was beating faster than a hummingbird's wings.

"Give me the reality. Better than the fantasy, I'll bet."

"Geoff, no..."

"What? You have other plans? How do you think Danny would react to seeing a tape of you on every laptop in the country?"

"You're a scumbag," I spat, my fear tempered by rage. "I knew we shouldn't have asked you back. Danny..."

"Danny, huh?" he growled. "Always Danny, isn't it, with you? Danny this, Danny that. Danny took my rightful place as head of the band. Took my place in your bed. You rejecting me over and over again just made me want you more. Then when I found out you held out for him, the guy who took my place as lead guitarist, it was the biggest blow. You thought you could screw me over for your precious Danny. But guess what, beautiful? I'm here – he's not. And you're mine now, not his..."

And then he lunged forward – a single, terrifying gesture. Before I could even scream, his hand was over my mouth. His enormous, hulking frame overpowering mine in a single instant. "Don't scream, Neve. Don't want to attract the wrong kind of attention."

"Geoff, stop it *right now*..."

But I was too late. He was too far gone. As effortlessly as if I were as light as a feather, he yanked my wrists and pulled me with him out the back door into the alleyway.

"Geoff, let me go!"

"You're coming with me, gorgeous..." His grin smelled of vomit.

I calculated my risks. Better scream than God knows what else. But he clapped a hand over my mouth and put a coat over my head. His body overpowered my own. I tried to struggle, to kick, to punch, to bite, but there was nothing I could do.

I could feel him dragging me forward, hear the tires of a car screeching to a halt.

"Grosvenor Hotel," he said. "And step on it."

And off we went, whirling into the night.

# Chapter 2

We sped through the streets of London. I was paralyzed by shock, fear – panic. Even at his lowest, at his sleaziest, Geoff had always been a friend to me, someone that I could, if not trust, nevertheless assume was never a threat to me. But that was the old Geoff. The Geoff I had known before the drugs, before the alcohol, before the hard living that had fried his brain. The Geoff that sat next to me in the cab, leering with a lascivious grin, pinching my inner thigh so hard that my skin turned black and blue, was a stranger to me. Drugs, alcohol, fast-living had turned him into someone else. My heart was pounding fast. Already we had left behind the O2 arena – already we were in a part of London I didn't recognize. I wanted to get out, to scream, to run, but something held me back. The tape that Geoff was talking about – was he bluffing? Did he really have a sex tape of me installed in my dorm room? My heart plummeted as I imagined that tape going viral, spread on every single video streaming platform between here and Tasmania. Imagined my father seeing it, my mother – imagined Danny watching it, his eyes full of pain and rage, silently judging me...

"You're one sick bastard, Geoff," I muttered.

"Maybe," Geoff looked sickly smug. "But I intend to get something out of this. You can't replace me without paying the price. I thought you were all my friends – but I was wrong. You're just out for yourselves, every last one of you. And I'm out for myself, too. Besides, I now know you weren't saving yourself. You're a slut like the others, like those girls who lined up after our performances just to have one night with a rock star, easy and ready to give it up to every last..."

I couldn't control my blinding anger. I'd wanted to stay cool, collected, in control. But in the moment I couldn't resist the urge to smack him – hard. My palm collided with the flat of his cheek, and the sharp stinging sound we made filled me with perverse pleasure.

"Everything all right back there, miss?" The cabbie turned around, worried.

"Everything's fine," Geoff said quickly. "She just likes playing a little rough, don't you, Never?" He grabbed my wrists tightly and whispered into my ear. "Unless you want that video uploaded to YouTube in ten seconds flat, I suggest you stay put."

I considered quickly. If I screamed and made a fuss now, the cabbie would likely get Geoff off me – but not before Geoff hit "send" on his cell phone and uploaded that video to the Internet. If we were heading back to Geoff's hotel – I'd be risking assault or worse. But I'd also be that much closer to his laptop – and to a team of security staff.

I had to think fast. "I'll be quiet," I said. "I'll do whatever you want, okay? Only one condition..."

"What?" Geoff's mouth widened as his perceived victory spread slowly, dully, across his face.

"I don't want to stay in the Grosvenor. It's stuffy and old-fashion. If we're going to do it, I want to do it somewhere...sexy." My own words repulsed me.

"Where do you want to go then, huh?" He took out his wallet, displaying a platinum credit card. "Anywhere you want, babe."

"The Mayfair Grand," I said quickly. *The Mayfair Grand Blue.* One of Danny's father's hotels. Somewhere

Danny would have access – somewhere he could get to us in time.

"The Mayfair Grand?" Geoff squeezed my thigh. "Girl has expensive tastes."

I wanted to throw up, but I kept my face calm.

"I'm cold," I said. "Give me your coat – I want to use it as a blanket."

"Trying to get my clothes off, huh? It's a shame to cover up those gorgeous legs of yours..." He moved his fingers further up my thigh, but relented and handed me his coat.

*Perfect.*

I moved my cell phone under the coat, hidden from view, and started typing, hoping I'd be able to use the touch pad without seeing. Texting Danny, Steve, everyone in my contacts list. *Emergency. MgrandBlue. Help me.*

Luckily, Geoff was too drunk to notice me sliding my cell phone back into my tiny purse. When we reached our destination, he threw a hundred-pound note at the cabbie and dragged me into the lobby. The moments passed by in a blur as he threw down his credit card at reception and dragged me into an elevator, up towards the penthouse suite...

"Sit on the bed," he grunted.

I followed orders, watching him warily. Now I just had to bide my time – hoping Danny had made it to Heathrow by now, that he had gotten my message. Geoff grinned at me. Instinctively, against myself, I felt a pang. Geoff had once been one of my dearest friends. I'd loved him once, the way I had loved Luc and Kyle and Steve. Never imagining that beneath that handsome exterior there lay demons. He'd been more gorgeous once, but his looks were ravaged by the effects of his hard living. Dark circles under his eyes. And that look of cruelty in his eyes that made me wonder if there was anything human in him any longer. Anything at all.

"Come on, Neve, take off your clothes or I'll take it off for you. I've only been wanting this since high school, you know. But you were off-limits, the legendary Keith Knight's daughter - pretty, popular without even trying, and always surrounded by guys, who you thought were friends. You were so into the music, so deep into the art, that you never notice how the guys all thought you were the hottest girl in school. A girl as hot as you, how can any guy just want to just be friends? We've all joined your band, hoping to get closer to you. Now you're all mine. Here." He shuddered, running his finger up and down my legs while I resisted kicking him. *The tape.* "But I haven't got all night."

"First, the video," I said, my voice shaking. "How do I know you're not bluffing – that you've even got one?"

"The video, huh?" Geoff laughed. "You want to see it? I've got it – tons of copies. I jerk off to it every single night – did you know that?"

I wanted to vomit. "You're crazy."

"I'm not crazy," Geoff said. "Just lucky. Lucky I got a glimpse of that nice, round ass. I always knew Keith Knight's daughter would have his full lips – and your mother's smoking body. I jacked off to loads of girls. Posters, images. Videos. But you I just needed to imagine. I remember seeing you naked and wet in the showers at camp when we were sixteen – and that one little slice of you was all I needed to imagine. But you'd never give me a chance, would you? Keith Knight's daughter was too good for any boy? Rock royalty, is that what you think you are? Untouchable? Unapproachable?"

"What the hell are you talking about, Geoff?" Deep down, I wanted to reason with him, to talk him down. To shake him out of this haze. "We're friends. We've always been friends. I never thought I was too good for you or anyone of my friends."

"I remember before I met you. I was a nobody. A geek. Like Steve. But being around you – it made all the guys notice. Girls, too. Thinking I was a somebody because I was hanging with Keith Knight's beautiful daughter. And then you think you can just drop me the second I get injured..."

"It wasn't just the injury, Geoff. It was the drugs..."

"Like your daddy dearest never did any?" he scoffed.

"Do you really want it like this, Geoff?" I asked, softly. "Me – not wanting you? Doing it because I have to?" *Just reason with him, Neve. Talk him down.* I reached over and brushed his cheek, trying to stifle the bile. "How are we supposed to work together after this? Don't you care about the band? Do you really want this?" His face softened for a moment and then he grew angry.

"This is *exactly* how I want this," he spat. "You finally forced off your high horse. Finally realizing that you're no better than a groupie slut. Realizing you're not some untouchable princess who can do whatever she wants just because of Daddy's money." His words stung. "This is exactly how I've fantasized about having you for so long." He grabbed my wrist. "On your back. Unable to resist. I watched you sing tonight, Neve. I wanted you so badly. I watched how your full lips nearly wrapped around the microphone and imagined your lips on me. I don't even have to touch you to get hard..."

"We're *friends*, Geoff." My voice was shaking. I knew now that what I was saying was untrue, had never been true. Whatever was wrong with Geoff, it had gone deep. Too deep. I couldn't save him. When did he stopped being friends and started objectifying me?

"And you think Kyle and Luc are your friends, too? Please, you're kidding yourself. They're hard as fuck over you, too – and you think by pretending to ignore it you can just lead them around like puppies, wrap them around your little finger. But I know you. Jessica Botano's daughter. Same soft silky hair. Same large tits. Same luscious ass."

"Geoff, stop it, now!"

"I know what you look like under those skimpy clothes you wear." He shoved his phone in front of my face. "I know who you are." He started playing a video. "This is just the beginning."

My mouth dropped open. I recognized the clip immediately. It was the morning I'd just come back from Danny's hotel room– I recognized the earrings. Recognized the way I'd taken off my bathrobe, my hair sopping wet from the shower, and looked at my naked body in the mirror as if for the first time. Looking at my body for the first time as an instrument, something capable of receiving and giving pleasure. Touching myself between my legs, closing my eyes in rapt ecstasy as I relived Danny's hands and tongue there. The most intimate, the most private moment in my life – captured on camera for Geoff to jerk off to. My facial expressions – at the moment expressions of pleasure – looked to me now ugly and ridiculous, shameful.

My cheeks burned with rage. "How dare you?" I said. "How fucking dare you?"

Geoff's hand was at his groin, softly rubbing, and his pants were unzipped. I wanted to be sick. And I knew then that no matter what Geoff did to me, no matter whom he showed the video to, I didn't care. There was no way I was going to spend another second in this room, another second with him. I grabbed the phone from his hand and threw it across the room, watching in sick delight as it shattered into hundreds of pieces on the floor.

"Careful, Neve. I told you I had copies."

"Erase them!" My voice was frenetic with rage. "All of them. Or I swear I'll rip out your balls and stuff them down your throat so far you're shitting them out. My father will make sure you never work again – make sure you can never use your cock again, you sick fuck..." I scoffed. "Go on, send that video. Send it to TMZ. And then when my family and I press charges, see how you like it in jail..."

"Neve..."

At that moment, the door flew open, and my whole body flooded with relief. Danny Blue was standing in the doorway, along with five of the burliest security guards I'd ever seen. He'd never looked more handsome and sexier than at that moment.

"Neve, thank God!" His voice was so soft, so tender, so loving, that tears filled my eyes.

The words started flowing out, all at once. "He got video of me – naked clips. Bugged my dorm room. Tried to blackmail..." But my voice failed me. As the security guys seized hold of Geoff, pinning him down, everything began to spin around me.

Then everything went black.

# Chapter 3

When I came to, I was resting in Danny's arms. He was holding me close... tenderly – almost gingerly, the way you would hold a baby bird. His fingers lightly stroked my hair. "Baby," he whispered. "Baby, what happened?"

"It was Geoff..." I spluttered. "He set up a hidden camera in the dorms before I moved to the apartment – to take footage of me. Of us. He threatened to send it to the tabloids unless I slept with him." My voice shook. "I thought if I could buy time – but Danny! You can't let him near his computer..."

"There's no danger of that," Danny said. "He tried to fight me. Fortunately, I've been trained in self-defense, and he was in no condition to fight. Knocked him out cold with a single punch. He's still unconscious. I'll have my dad's security check out his computer, see what we can find." His voice was professional, almost cold around the security he brought. When they left, and we were alone then the emotion broke in, all at once. "That scumbag!" he exclaimed. "That absolute prick. He had no right – to violate you like that..."

"If you hadn't come..." I shuddered. "He wanted to rape me – he said so himself." My whole mouth tasted like vomit. "I can't work with him anymore – I won't!"

"We can call the police – press charges..."

I shook my head. "And get negative publicity for the band right after our first big show?" I sighed. "No, no – just get him away from me. For good. That's all I want. To forget."

Danny held me tighter. "I'm so sorry, babe," he whispered. "If I hadn't stepped down, if I hadn't left the band, this never would have happened. I should have stayed by you."

I reached up and brought his face down to mine, kissing him softly. "Don't worry," I said. "It's not your fault. We should have found someone new – shouldn't have asked him back..." I traced my fingers along his cheeks. "I missed you, Danny. It's been weeks."

"I know," he groaned. "I'm so sorry for what happened, Neve..."

### Never Land (The Never Knights #2)

"He thought I'd be with him. After everything he did. He thought he could force me to have sex with him – that I'd just let him have his way with me, after everything..."

"My men searched him after we knocked him out," said Danny. "That fellow has more drugs on his person than your average dealer in Camden. Heroin, cocaine, ketamine. He wasn't himself – that's for sure. That man you saw tonight wasn't your friend. He wasn't the Geoff you knew."

"He was a monster," I said.

"Or a very, very sick man," he replied. "It's why I don't do drugs," he said. "I know the harm it can do..." I knew he was thinking of Peyton, of his old life, and my heart sank.

"I got us another room," Danny said softly, leading me lightly by the hand out of the room. "We don't have to do anything, not after what you've been through. Don't worry. We can go to sleep, side by side. I'll be holding you. That's what I want to do, just hold you safely against my chest." He used his key card and swiped us into a gorgeous suite, floor-to-ceiling windows overlooking the London Eye.

"Danny..." I tried to control my voice. I was shaken, still in shocked at what could've happened with Geoff. "What happened with Geoff. It made me feel dirty, filthy. Like I'd lost control." I looked up at him. "But with you – I feel in control. All the time. Even when you make me scream...or moan. I feel safe. I want to feel safe again, right now. With you." I gulped. "I want you to make me feel safe having sex with a man again and not disgust."

He looked up at me, his eyes shining with longing. "Are you sure, Neve?" He brought his finger up to my chin so I would look him straight in the eye. "We don't have to, and I'm fine with just holding you all night."

"I want to choose what I do with my body." I smiled playfully. "And with yours."

He kissed the top of my head and smiled gently. "Lie back," he said. He hiked up my leather dress so that it reached my stomach. "Black panties," he said, kissing the border of my lingerie. "My favorite."

"I wore it just for you," I murmured, as he lightly tugged them off my hips, taking them into his teeth as he pulled them off my body.

### Never Land (The Never Knights #2)

"Of course," he whispered, "my favorite of all is with you wearing nothing at all underneath..." He worked his tongue back up towards my inner thighs, making me shudder. "Just tell me if you want me to stop, Neve."

"I won't tell you to stop..."

When we woke up to the soft morning light streaming in through the window, Danny and I were both covered in sweat. The morning felt glorious. My whole body ached – but the ache was not painful. Rather, it was the sensation of all my muscles relaxed at once for the first time in a month. Relief spreading through my veins. Even after the stress of last night, Danny had been able to bring me to screaming climax not once but three times in the course of the evening, delaying his own pleasure until the very end. I'd learned that the sight of his face, rapt in ecstasy, the feeling of his body shuddering beneath my own, the sound of his soft moans – these things were almost as pleasurable to me as the orgasms he gave me. His body against mine – his pleasure became my own.

I leaned over and took him all in. His long, ebony-dark hair streaked with sweat, falling around his shoulders, a dark nimbus surrounding his preternaturally beautiful features. There was almost something androgynous about his face, his enormous blue eyes, his full, plush lips. But his body was decidedly masculine. Rock-hard abs, chiseled hips that framed his perfectly-formed shaft. Immediately I tensed up with desire for him. I wrapped my arms around him, pressing my lips against his shoulder, lightly tracing my tongue up and down his chest.

"Here," he said in a low, gravelly voice. "Use this." He lightly stroked a peacock feather up and down my naked body, making me shiver. "It was in the vase on the coffee table. But I figured we could put it to...less decorative uses." My body tingled all over.

Clearly morning hadn't limited Danny's stamina. Immediately he was all over me, cupping my breasts with his lips, lightly kneading my flesh with his fingers so that it ached, just slightly, with a glorious pain that only intensified the pleasure. He had me screaming in seconds, my thighs quivering at his touch, as his nimble fingers found the spots that made me writhe when brushed, licked, sucked upon. Before I knew it I was dozing in his arms again, exhausted and drained, the bedsheets smelling of sweet sweat.

**Never Land (The Never Knights #2)**

Danny's eyes were closed as he lay next to me, his gaze peaceful at last, his long lashes closed. *Do you still have nightmares?* I wondered. Did he still dream of Peyton, the girl he had once loved, the girl whose death had broken something deep within him? I longed to comfort him, to hold him, to wipe away his tears, to take away that pain...

"Get some sleep, love," he moaned. "You'll need it. You won't get much today"

"Aren't we done for the day?"

"Not even close..." He grinned. "When have you ever known me to last only a couple of rounds?" This time he focused solely on my breasts, leaving the area between my legs untouched as he cupped my breasts in his hands, lightly tonguing my nipples. The sensation was new to me, gloriously strange – my body was so sensitive by now that even this slight touch was enough to make me arch my back and moan aloud.

"Danny..." I cried his name out over and over again.

We were wrapped in each other's arms, kissing each other slowly, tortuously slowly, when there came a knock at the door.

Immediately we sprang to our feet, putting on the black silk dressing gowns the hotel had provided for us. I opened the door to find a familiar female face. It was Cassandra Curry, meticulously dressed as ever in couture garments that seamlessly blended fashion and professionalism. Her eyes fell on Danny first.

"I was actually looking for Neve," she said, flushing slightly. I could see her react with faint pleasure to the sight of Danny's magnificent tanned abs peeking through the gown.

"I'm here," I said.

Her eyes went back and forth to me and him.

"I've been trying to reach you and Geoff all morning," she said. "The photoshoot with Rolling Stone this afternoon has been pushed up to one o'clock – we need to get you into hair and makeup, pronto. Where's Geoff?"

My heart sank once more. How was I going to explain to Cassandra that Geoff had to go – no matter what?

"He can't make it," I said quickly. "Plastered."

"I don't care if he's throwing up on the carpet, Neve – this is the cover shoot for Rolling Stone. The whole band needs to be there. You know that." She gave me a stern, almost maternal look. Clearly Cassandra was used to dealing with difficult rock stars. "I'll tell you what I told Jagger. You can throw up just out of frame."

"We can't have him there, Cassandra," I said.

"Why not? Is he dead?" She rolled her eyes. "Even then, I'm sure the make-up department can make him look presentable."

"I just...can't deal with him right now," I said, my heart pounding. "Look, some pretty serious stuff's gone down with Geoff – and I'm not sure how we're going to stay together after this."

Cassandra looked unimpressed. "I don't take kindly to band drama, Neve," she said. "Whatever this is, this had better be good."

"Cassie, Geoff's a liability. He made a sex tape of me without my knowledge and threatened to send it to the tabloids last night unless I slept with him."

Cassandra looked shocked. "Fifteen years in this business," she said. "Since I was eighteen. And I've never heard something so disgusting in my life. I thought you were all so close..."

"We were," I said grimly. "But Geoff – it's not just the drugs or the booze. Something's wrong with him.

Seriously wrong. It's like he's a different person. Don't tell me you haven't been worried about him..."

Cassandra sighed. "I've got my work cut out for me today. I don't care if he's at fault – the second the words "sex tape" hit the press some hacker, *someone* will get hold of it, deleted or not. And it's bad for your image. You don't need me to tell you that. If you want him out of the band, I'll have to come up with a pretty bloody good cover story to protect all of your asses. Including my own. Do you definitely want him out of the band?"

I knew I did – but I also knew that *Rolling Stone* was preparing a studio for us halfway across town. For all of us. "Can we get the rest of the band over?" I said. "I figured it was best they heard the story direct from me."

"Don't worry, Neve," Danny said, cradling me in his arms. "Listen – the second Geoff sobers up, he'll be so ashamed and so relieved not to be in a jail cell he'll drop out of the band of his own accord."

Cassie looked over at Dan. "Who's this?"

"Cassie, meet Danny Blue."

Her eyes widened. "Your old guitarist?" She looked impressed, looking back and forth between me and him, clearly taking in the situation. "I *see...*"

No sooner had Kyle, Luc, and Steve arrived than I explained to them the situation. Luc and especially Kyle were distinctly awkward around Danny – even changing into a crisp white T-shirt and jeans had not gotten rid of Danny's decidedly "post-coital" messy look – and Danny picked up on the fact instantly. "Listen, Neve," he said. "I've got to go see my father about some business – why don't I let you sort all this out with your band mates without getting in the way?" He kissed me lightly on the lips and out of the corner of my eye I could see Kyle tense as Danny walked away. Kyle and Luc were both glowering, but once I had explained to them about Geoff, their whole expressions changed.

"The asshole!" Kyle exploded. "The absolute asshole! How dare he!"

"Where is he?" said Steve. "We're going to give him one hell of a *talking-to*." He clenched his fists.

"With security," I said. "They've already questioned him. They're working on the laptop now." I sighed. "But we have to decide what to do," I said. "About the band. About our guitarist. In time for the shoot."

"Let's go pay Geoff a visit," Luc said. "Shall we?"

# Chapter 4

A knock came at the door. Luc and I started. "Are we expecting anyone?" I asked Cassie, who shrugged.

"I hope not," said Cassandra. "I can't deal with any more surprises today. Already I have about ninety minutes to tell *Rolling Stone* that either the Never Knights is short its lead guitarist or that he's somehow failed to materialize for their shoot." She sighed deeply. "Look, there's one thing I can do to buy time – but that's all. I can suggest that we do the shoot in the hotel. A sort of candid "rockers behind closed doors" sort of thing. If they agree to hold it here at least that will save you time getting across London..." She didn't look too thrilled. "But I'm warning you – all of you. I don't tolerate too much distraction in this line of work. My job is to make sure you turn a profit for the record label regardless of your rocker partying – and I've seen plenty of bands just as talented as you burn out through drama and drink before they'd even had their fifteen minutes. RRR wants to support your careers – but don't sabotage them."

"No, I understand," I said, flushing. The last thing I wanted to do was make Cassandra think we were anything but professional. "This won't happen again." I went to answer the door. Before me stood a very elegant older gentleman wearing a perfectly tailored Saville Row suit. "Hotel management," he said, his accent dripping with world-weary disdain. "The...gentleman in question has been detained by hotel security after a rather riotous night. Mr. Blue has instructed me to take you to him, although I doubt he's in any condition to be of much explanatory use to you."

The man led me and the rest of the band down a flight of stairs and across a corridor. Located in the walls, almost imperceptible, was a door that led us into a control room filled with monitors. "Security," he said lightly, leading us through the room and into the staff quarters, rooms far simpler in scale than the grand suites upstairs. Geoff was lying on one of the plain white beds. He looked utterly miserable. His eyes were blood-shot, and his face was bathed in sweat; the whole room and his clothing smelled of vomit. Geoff was holding an ice pack to his jaw, hyperventilating. When he saw me he stumbled to his feet, still dizzy and reeling from the drugs.

"Neve..." he breathed. "Neve, I'm so sorry, but..."

Luc and Kyle looked ready to snap, but to my surprise it was Steve who leaped forward, fury written clear on his face. "Save it," he said, punching Geoff clear in the guts, causing him to double over in pain and stumble back on the bed. "Listen to me, asshole," Steve's face had gone bright red, and his jaw was contorted in a look of pure rage. He pulled up Geoff's shirt, dragging Geoff back to his feet, and threw him against a wall. Geoff moaned loudly as Steve smashed his body against the wall repeatedly, pummeling. "Don't you ever go near her again, asshole!" Steve shouted. "Do you understand me? Do you? Do you?" His face was the color of a red, ripe tomato. "Got it?"

"Steve, cool down!" I cried, trying to pull Steve off Geoff. I was shocked. Off all of us, Steve was always the coolest head, the calmest voice in the room. The only one not to succumb to the band drama that had seemed to engulf us lately. But now I saw a different side of Steve. He'd finally snapped, finally lost control, whaling on Geoff like a punching bag. "Come on," I said, grabbing Steve by the back of the shirt. "He's not a threat to me anymore – let security deal with it." I looked at Kyle and Luc. They were friends of Geoff's – or were, at any rate. They'd know how to deal with him. "You two talk to him," I said. "I can't look at him right now."

"Sorry, Neve," Steve said when we were outside, still shaking with anger. His fists were clenched and his face was still blazing. "I didn't mean to lose it like that. I was just so angry."

"It's okay," I pulled Steve in for a hug. "Believe me, I was so mad at him I wanted to do the exact same thing. It was hard for me to restrain myself. But the last thing we want is more gossip – I'm just trying to get past it..."

"I just..." Steve was still gaping, in shock. "I trusted him. I knew him. I felt safe around him – he was a *friend.* I never thought he'd hurt you – or any of us – like that. Especially you. You're like family to me, and I keep thinking...how could he do something so vile, so evil? You're more than family to me, Neve. You're like the sister I never had. You're my sister. There's no way any guy could do what he did to you and not hear from me..."

### Never Land (The Never Knights #2)

"Well," I said grimly, "I guess I don't have to worry about that tape getting out after all. If Geoff so much as accesses Facebook I know you guys will pummel him before he can leak the video. But still..." I exhaled sharply. "I thought of him as a friend, Steve. I really did. I trusted him, too. And what he did to me...it was awful."

"I know," said Steve darkly. "We all feel that way. That's what hurts. And what he did to you – or try to do to you – it's disgusting. I know we all joke about the rock star lifestyle – about losing control. But that's different. The girls I go with – I respect them, and they respect me. It's consensual, always. Even if a girl's drunk, I'd never...but with Geoff, it's like he gets off on the power of...I can't say the word." He looked up at me. "No real man has to do that to get with a girl – no matter what. I have no respect for any guy who has to force it."

"I'm just glad Danny got there in time," I said. "Even if I'd been able to get to the laptop, or convince him not to send the video – who's to say he wouldn't have resorted to violence, to force..." Just the thought of Geoff on top of me, his eyes filled with hatred and lust, disgusted me. Steve saw my stricken face and pulled me in close for another hug. "I may pretend to be a ladies' man onstage,

Neve, but I'm a gentleman. All of us are – except for that loser Geoff. None of us would ever hurt you like that, believe me." He paused. "But, about that tape..."

"Danny's security team is going through his computer right now."

"When we get back home, we can search his apartment too." He laughed bitterly. "To think, we used to play poker at that place every other night."

"I know. It's crazy." I looked up. "Then...what about the band?"

"What about the band?"

"Are we keeping Geoff?"

Steve's eyes bugged out of his head. "Of course not, Neve! How could you even think we'd do that to you? After what Geoff did he's lucky he doesn't end up in prison. I'd never put you in harm's way like that..."

"But the shoot today. And the performance tomorrow. How are we supposed to find a new lead before that?" I smiled sadly. "Here we are again, huh."

"There *is* someone who knows all the songs. Who could play for us at a moment's notice – no audience required," Steve grinned.

### Never Land (The Never Knights #2)

"Danny?"

Steve nodded. "He's here, he knows how to wield a guitar, and he's *good*, Neve."

"And what about Kyle and Luc?" I said. "The whole reason Danny left the band is because of them."

"We can work on that," said Steve. "Time's passed. Both have had time to cool off. And Kyle really hit it off with one of the girls we met last night – turns out they both love Goth rock. He's taking her to the Siouxsie reunion show next week..."

I smiled with relief. So Kyle was moving on. His single-minded obsession with me was cooling down a bit. But still...I couldn't help but feel a pang. I'd come to take for granted Kyle's feelings for me, his loyalty and his kindness. Had he really forgotten about me so quickly? I knew I could never return Kyle's feelings, not with Danny in the picture, but what would have happened with him if he'd made his confession before I'd met Danny? Or if Luc...?

"And is Luc doing okay?" I asked. Luc – whom I have always thought of as a close friend, and yet who always gave me a strange tingle when we touched, a gentle spark. Like the night we sat together on the porch swing after Geoff was injured. Luc and I – had we had *something* going on? Something that had never quite come to fruition? I thought about Luc's kindness, his warmth, his enormous loving Italian family – would they have come to treat me like one of them, if I was Luc's girlfriend? Another road not taken.

Steve shook his head. "I know he's still having a kind of hard time with things," he said. "I should know; I'm his roommate. But in a way I'm less worried about him than Kyle. He's older, more mature. He's dated a lot of girls. He'll be able to put on a brave face for the team more easily than Kyle will. But he's not over it." He leaned in. "He's wanted this since junior high, Neve, and when you guys kissed apparently he thought you really liked him. When he found out about you and Danny he went out drinking, came back home drunk, punching the wall. He didn't want to talk about it too much, but he was really upset."

My mouth fell open. Until a few weeks ago, I didn't even know that Luc liked me like that – and now to find out he'd liked me for years! "I didn't know it was that deep."

"He's had it bad for a while. Since the eighth grade."

### Never Land (The Never Knights #2)

"Then why didn't he say anything?" *Why hadn't I noticed anything?* I thought about Luc, about his sweet smile, his kind eyes, his handsome face. He'd always been so wonderful around me, so attentive and loving – but he'd never let on that his feelings were anything more than genuine friendship. "Don't answer that..." I didn't want to hear the truth. That Luc had held off out of respect for the band – something I'd been unable to do. "I have to talk to Luc," I said. I turned back towards the door. "But first, I need to deal with Geoff."

I returned to the room to see Kyle and Luc in Geoff's face, questioning him about the video. He looked utterly defeated, filthy and exhausted in the harsh light of day. They stared at him with anger in their eyes.

Geoff staggered to his feet. "Neve, I'm so sorry...I fucked up, I know that. I was off my face last night. I'd taken every drug in the book. Listen, I'll get clean, I'll get sober, I promise. Only...I don't want to leave knowing I didn't apologize to you. I don't want to go through life regretting that I didn't."

"You, you, you," said Kyle loudly. "It's always about you, isn't it?"

"Just Neve...please..." Geoff reached out towards me. "Don't press charges. I can't have a criminal record, I just can't! This will follow me for the rest of my life – I'll be ruined..."

I felt sick. Even now, all Geoff could think about was himself. And I knew I couldn't waste another second of my life thinking about him. "You're not staying in jail," I said, turning away so I didn't have to see his face. "You don't have to worry about that. But if you don't delete every one of those tapes, you'll wish to God you never knew me. Now get out of my face. You find your own flight home."

# Chapter 5

Security escorted Geoff out, and Cassie folded her arms. "Right," she said. "You're better off without him, if that little display was anything to go by. Now, what am I going to do about RRR?"

"Brief them that Geoff's gone," said Steve. "Tell them they'll have a replacement within the hour – in time for the photo-shoot."

"Who?"

"That's confidential," said Steve. Cassie looked perplexed, but shrugged and left. Luc, Kyle and Steve started walking out. I knew what I had to do.

"Hey Luc," I said. "Do you want to grab a quick breakfast or something?"

He turned around, surprised.

"Yeah, sure," he said, coming up to me. He patted me on the shoulder. "How are you doing, Neve? Are you okay?"

"I've been better," I admitted, "but it's a lot easier being here among friends. Better now."

"Neve..." Luc turned to me. "What he did was unconscionable. You and I know that. He took advantage of you in the worst way possible."

"He made me feel so violated..."

"Nobody could violate you," said Luc. "What he tried to do shamed him, not you." He leaned in close, so that his words tickled my ear. "When I found out what he'd tried to do, I just saw red. Neve, you know my dad's high up in the force. Just got a promotion to Captain. If you do want to press charges..."

"I think Danny's security guys have done what needed doing," I said, and I saw a look of pain flash across Luc's face. I bit my lip and inwardly kicked myself. There I was again – unintentionally hurting Luc by reminding him of Danny. "I mean...security here already went through his laptop, and I don't want to press charges..."

"I know," said Luc. "But when we're back in the US, you'll want to feel safe there, too. I just want to help." When he looked at me with those enormous, puppy-brown eyes, it took my breath away. I loved Danny – but I couldn't deny that the sight of those stunning irises made me swoon a little. I'd never thought of Luc as a romantic interest before – or of anyone else, for that matter, but somehow knowing Luc's feelings for me made me reassess the past, reassess our history. Had I just taken his beauty, his stunning charisma, for granted all these years?

"Let's get that breakfast," I said. "Just us. To talk."

"Sure," he said.

The breakfast room at the hotel was full, but Luc smiled at the hostess and soon we found ourselves sitting at the best seat in the house.

"I see your charm works wonders abroad as well as at home," I tried to tease.

"To some extent, Neve." Luc gave me a slow smile. "But not where it matters most," he added softly.

"Luc," I reached forward to take his hand. "I just wanted to talk – to apologize for not telling you about Danny sooner. I wanted to keep it a secret from the band, and at first I thought it was just...not a serious thing. Something I wanted to keep private. I didn't know how you felt – I really didn't, not until..."

*Until we kissed.*

"What I felt for Danny, it surprised me, too. I couldn't believe it. It's not that I don't like you or find you attractive. I do – on both counts. And if circumstances were different, maybe..."

"Don't say that," Luc said, inhaling slowly, letting out his breath through his teeth. "Don't give me false hope. Don't say maybe. I can't deal with that."

"Luc..."

"Neve," Luc said firmly. "It's okay. I get it. You don't like me that way. I'm a grown-up. I'll get over it. I'm not like Kyle, who's so attached to you – or like Geoff, who thinks he can force you into wanting him. I'm sure there's a lot of guys out there who are going to have to get over you not wanting them – anyone with eyes in their head would want you."

I couldn't help but laugh. "This whole time, I had no idea."

"Since we formed the band. Since you and I met at Camp Summerside. But I was stupid. I was shy..."

"I wish you'd told me earlier," I said.

"But I didn't," Luc said. "There's no point looking back. I believe in fate and destiny. If we were meant to be, we'd be. And if not..." He threw up his hands. "It's not going to be easy for me, but I'll live. As long as you're happy." He looked into my eyes. *"Are* you happy?"

I nodded. "Yes," I said slowly.

Luc pursed his lips. "Then I'll just have to get used to it – if I want to keep you in my life."

"There's just one thing, Luc," I said.

"What?"

"Danny. With Geoff out of the band, we need a new lead..."

Luc visibly flinched. "Right," he said. "And Danny's our best bet at such short notice. He's better than Geoff, that's for sure. More talented."

"Then you agree?"

Luc considered. "Just...be sensitive," he said. "If you can. The two of you. It's going to be hard seeing you...be romantic with each other around me."

"No PDA during band time, got it."

"Just let's keep it professional."

"I'll be a pro, like always, Luc. You don't have to worry about that." I touched Luc's hands lightly, and felt his fingers twine around mine, a feeling that sent electric shocks through my body.

"I love you Neve," Luc said abruptly before looking away.

I closed my eyes. Whatever Luc said, I knew he'd have a hard time with accepting Danny in the band. His words made my whole body ache.

"Luc," I tried to get the words out. "I care for you too. As a friend..."

"Neve," Luc said. "Danny is the best guitarist out there. And if I set my feelings for you aside for the good of the band, I'll do it wholeheartedly. Danny's a good guy, and I'll do what I have to do to keep my own feelings from ruining the band for all of us."

I smiled up at him.

"Thank you," I whispered.

As I approached Kyle and Steve's room, I heard hushed voices. Apparently Kyle and Steve were already having the conversation about Danny's future in the band without me. Eager to hear what was being said, I leaned against the ajar door.

"Look, we don't have time to hold auditions," Steve was saying. "And even if we did – it would be bad publicity. It would look like we didn't have control of the situation."

"So who do we get? We can't work with Geoff again!"

"Danny Blue, that's who." Steve chuckled softly.

"*Danny,*" Kyle almost spat out the name. "Is that really our only option? I mean, he's not a bad guy or anything, but don't you think we can find someone who..."

"Kyle..." Steve's voice was soft, almost gentle. "You're going to have to get over the fact that Neve is dating someone. Sooner or later you'll have to move on. And do you really want to let your personal life interfere with the band."

"*Her* personal life is interfering with the band!" Kyle insisted. But he stopped and sighed. "I know I'm being ridiculous," he said. "But it's hard."

"If you screw up the band, Kyle, you'll risk losing her altogether. As a friend and as something more. If the band implodes, that's it. For all of us. If you want to be in her life – in *any* of our lives – the thing to do is move on."

We were interrupted by the appearance of Cassandra Curry, who strode past us straight into the hotel room, followed by a photographer and a whole team of makeup artists. "Guys," she said simply. "The good news is, *Rolling Stone* has agreed to having the shoot here. The bad news is, it's happening now. What's the final verdict on Geoff? If he's gone, then it's time to improvise. I want to know who this controversial new replacement is that Steve's been on about."

"Geoff's gone," I said.

"Then who's the replacement?" Cassie asked. "He'd better be hot – Geoff was getting tons of panty-dropping fan-mail, and the new guy's got to match a pretty tough fan base. Not to mention good, of course. You've got a performance tomorrow night to prepare for."

"It's Danny," I said. "Danny Blue. Our old guitarist. He's back."

As if on command, Danny appeared in the corridor, having been summoned by my text. "What's going on?" He looked around in confusion at the team of artists and photographers prepping the hotel suite.

Cassie looked him up and down. "At least he's got the hot part covered," she said. "I'll wait and see how the talent turns out. Does he *always* look that good?"

### Never Land (The Never Knights #2)

My mouth opened in a surprised O at her words. "Yeah, basically."

She looked at me sternly. "Then he'd better be worth risking a band over. If your history with him goes south...a band can only go through so many replacements in the early months."

"It won't go south."

"Ah, youth," Cassie said dryly. "It must be good to be young."

Danny came over to me and grabbed my hands, pulling me in for a kiss. Mindful of Kyle and Luc, I did my best to pull away, signaling him that we should act with more subtlety.

"So what am I doing here?" Danny said. "Your text said it was important. Is it Geoff?"

"No," I said. "You're in the shoot."

"I'm *what*?"

"*Rolling Stone*. They're prepping the room now. That girl in the corner will be handling your makeup."

Danny gaped. "What? When did that happen?"

"When you became the lead guitarist of the Never Knights."

"Are you saying...?"

"Geoff...resigned, shall we say. And we need an emergency guitarist."

Danny was stunned. "But what about..." he looked over at Luc and Kyle.

"It's fine," I said. "They've cooled down. We all have. We've agreed it's the best thing for the band. If it's what you want."

Danny didn't need to take too much time to consider. "Let's rock and roll," he said, leaning into my ears. "Anything that means I get to spend more time with you is a good thing," he whispered. "Because last night? That was just a prelude..."

# Chapter 6

Immediately the room flooded with people. Before Danny or I could move, what seemed like dozens of makeup artists, photographers, and on-site coordinators were swarming into the room, setting up camera tripods, bringing in rack after rack of costumes, carrying enormous boxes and suitcases.

"Wow," Steve's jaw dropped. "This is insane, guys. Look..."

We all looked around, utterly fascinated by what we saw. Row after row of the most beautiful clothes I'd ever seen, gorgeous black satin gowns and white lace, couture red velvet and damask silk, spikes, chains, military jackets.

"We were able to borrow some costumes from the National Theater," explained Cassie. "We want to have a costume theme. Sort of – playing dress-up, kids trying on new clothes, that kind of feel."

I reached out to touch the silk, feeling its smoothness against my fingers. My whole body was tingling with excitement. This was the most luxurious hotel suite I'd ever been in, and these people around me...they were the sort of people I'd associated with my dad's life. With rock stars and fame and fortune. Not with a college band that two months ago had been rehearsing in Luc's mom's basement and living off frozen pizzas. And now, suddenly, here we were. Being primped and prepared for a shoot with *Rolling Stone.* I wasn't sure whether to be overjoyed or overwhelmed. Did this mean we'd made it? That now, finally, people were starting to see the Never Knights as a band with the promise to make it big? A gorgeous brunette with sparkling green eyes took hold of me and sat me down in a chair, gripping me firmly by the shoulders.

"Makeup time," she said cheerily. "We've got a lot of work to do with you. I've got a very special idea."

"What is it?" I asked, slightly confused at the sheer colorful array of pencils and brushes she was getting out.

"You'll see," the woman said. "I've done a lot of makeup chairs in the past few months, but I've got to say – this is one of the most exciting. It's not often that you get hype like this." She looked over at Cassandra, who was authoritatively barking out directions on her cell phone. "Your PR manager is good at her job. She knows how to create a buzz, that's for sure." She made me close my eyes as she started applying makeup to my face, painting it with what felt like sticky goo. Meanwhile, a second attendant was changing my clothes, putting on a tight-fitting jacket and pants on, moving me around to avoid getting in the makeup artist's way.

"Keep your eyes closed," the makeup artist said. "You'll see the whole costume when it's done."

If I turned slightly pink at the idea that I was changing in front of an entire room full of people, the makeup probably hid it.

"Okay, surprise," chirped the makeup artist. "You can open your eyes now."

When I looked into the mirror, my mouth fell wide open with shock. Standing before me was a mirror image of Captain Beam – my father's most famous onstage persona. The glam rock space captain, with spiky blond hair and a painted lightning bolt covering his face from his meticulously painted eyes to his dark-red lips, who had caused an entire generation of screaming 70's fan girls to become obsessed with androgyny. Captain Beam had lasted my father through two platinum-selling albums and several additional singles; whenever he launched a reunion tour, Captain Beam was always his most popular character. And here I was, my hair spiked up and frosted slightly with spray-in dye, the familiar lightning bolt across my eyes, the green eye-shadow, the dark lips. Even my clothes were the same, albeit, a sexed-up, more feminine version of the spikey-shouldered jacket and form-fitting leather pants Captain Beam had worn.

My heart sank as I realized what all this meant. *Rolling Stone* didn't just want the Never Knights on the cover, they wanted me – Neve Knight, Keith Knight's daughter.

I looked around and saw that the other band members were being dressed in identical long black-leather coats with blue eyeliner. The same costumes the members of Captain Beam's Galaxy Band used to wear.

"What's all this?" I looked around, confused.

"We want to recreate all of Keith Knight's classic looks," Cassie explained. "Only – with you in the leading role. Captain Beam. The Lonely Walker. All of them."

"So this is about my father..." my voice wavered.

### Never Land (The Never Knights #2)

"It's our biggest selling point," said Cassie. "Remember, these guys in *Rolling Stone* have grown up with Keith and Jessica. They've seen your baby pictures. They already know you as the girl Keith Knight wrote "Midnight Lullaby" for. There's no getting around it. Everyone wants to know if Keith Knight's daughter can live up to his image. And this way, they'll see that you can rock the same outfits – even sexier than the King of Glam himself."

"But what about the other band members?"

"They'll be in the shot, don't worry. But you're our focus."

"But our music?"

"People want to see you, Neve. You're the draw right now. Once we get bums in seats and start shifting stock, then people will listen to your music. But we have to get them to bite, first."

My stomach plummeted. So, this was how it was going to be. No matter how much I tried to make a name for myself, no matter how many times I tried to be independent and establish the Never Knights as an independent entity, my father's name and legacy would always haunt us.

Luckily for me, the other band members seemed not to mind – or if they did, they pretended not to. They cheerfully allowed the team of makeup artists to fuss over and primp them, painting on false birthmarks, adding synthetic eyelashes and plenty of eyeliner. Everyone looked painfully, mind-numbingly gorgeous. Just looking at the four of them in a room – angelic, sensitive Kyle, brooding, dark-eyed Luc, charming, charismatic Steve and of course Danny, whose gorgeous looks were only accentuated by the skillful professionalism of the makeup artist – made me want to melt. No wonder we always had female groupies hanging out around us – I was surrounded by four of the best-looking guys on the planet.

"Hey, look!" Kyle laughed. "More costumes!" He pulled out a rack of military jackets – part of my father's Soviet Soldier phase in the late '80's.

"Is this Lenin or Lonely Hearts' Club?" Luc laughed as he put on a tight-fitting military jacket from the Soviet era. "These costumes are great!"

It warmed my heart to see them all so happy, so enthusiastic.

### Never Land (The Never Knights #2)

Danny came up behind me and squeezed my hand as unobtrusively as he could manage. He, at least, had picked up on my discomfort. "Don't worry about it," he said. "Captain Beam or not – you look beautiful. And it won't take long before you show the world that you're not just your father's daughter. You're a talented, ambitious, exciting new voice in your own right. Don't forget that."

His words made me smile. I squeezed his hand right back, enjoying the feel of his flesh against mine.

"Let's do this!" Cassie shouted, and immediately the five of us were posing on the bed, the flashbulbs going off in our faces as the camera *clicked* loudly. Photograph after photograph was taken – each time we moved, turned, posed, writhed like cats. One costume and then the next – Soviet military jackets, spiky metal collars, the pseudo-preppy look of my father's Lonely Walker album. Soon I let go of my misgivings and allowed myself to enjoy it – enjoy being center stage, mugging for the cameras, laughing and joking with the boys as the camera caught our every move.

By the time we finished the shoot it was evening, and we were all exhausted and hungry.

"What do you say we hit up Shoreditch?" Steve suggested. "Apparently it's the cool place to go if you want to get away from all the snobs this side of town. They've got some great bars – and the drinking age is 18! No need for fake Ids."

Kyle and Luc enthusiastically agreed, before turning to me and Danny.

"Guys?" Luc asked, trying hard to be friendly to both of us. I could see how difficult it was for him; his eyes still welled up with ink-dark pain.

"Actually..." Danny said. "Do you mind if we catch up with you later? I have to talk to Neve about something – is that fine by you, Neve?"

I nodded and bid farewell to the others. "What is it?"

"How about we go for a drive?" Danny grinned at me. He led me down into the hotel lobby and out into the street, where a shiny silver Aston Martin awaited us.

"Your ride?" I asked.

"All mine," Danny spun the keys around in his hand and opened the door for me. "You first, love."

"So where are we going? A scenic ride through the countryside? A trip to the West End?" I'd eagerly read my

London guidebook, and I was set to see as much of the city's tourist sites as possible before we headed home.

"I'd hoped to take you to one of my favorite restaurants, a Sushi place in South Kensington," said Danny. "But...my father changed all that." He visibly tensed at the mention of his father.

I looked up at him. "What about your father?"

"I met with him earlier today. And...well...." he stiffened. "Dad wants to meet you. He asked if we'd meet him at his nightclub in Chelsea. Not really our sort of place – too stuck up. But he wants to get to know you." He rolled his eyes.

"What's so wrong with that?" I asked.

"You don't know my father," he said. "He had a thing for Jessica Botano, quite seriously. When she won Swimsuit Model of the Year he tried to hire her to come out of a birthday cake for his 50th birthday celebrations. I was quite young at the time..."

I made a face. "You think he'll be...a bit creepy?"

"He's a 'bit creepy' as you call it with everyone. That's just his natural personality." Danny grimaced. "Whether it's just that he wants to ogle the famous Botano genes or he wants to embarrass me in public, I don't trust the situation. My father rarely invites me – or a significant other – to anything but a business function without some ulterior motive. And the last thing I want is for you to get mixed up in all of that. And of course, I'll have to see my father's latest child-bride. Veronica Taylor. The former reality star. Have you heard of her?"

"I've seen her ads." She was the current face of Dior perfumes – an ethereally gorgeous, pallid young woman. "Isn't she like thirteen?"

"Twenty-one," said Danny. "They've already been married six months...she's the youngest one yet."

"Careful," I said, trying to lighten the mood. "They're getting younger and younger. The next one won't be out of high school yet."

"She's five years younger than me," said Danny. "Which is thoroughly strange." He sighed. "Well, Roni is *lively*, certainly. I suppose she keeps my daddy dearest young."

I looked over at Danny again. His face was still, stony. Almost expressionless.

We turned on to King's Road and headed towards the river, where some elegant lights greeted us to BLUE

**Never Land (The Never Knights #2)**

WATER, the waterside branch of Danny's father's London empire. Barges were laid out on the Thames, and people in haute couture and sumptuous coats were standing or sitting and drinking next to pulsing heat lamps.

"Ready to meet the dragon?" Danny turned to me.

I gulped. "Ready," I said.

# Chapter 7

No sooner had we walked in than I began to feel as if I were under a microscope. Everyone stopped and turned to stare at us; voices hushed as we approached, and I felt everyone in the bar stop in order to size me up, looking me up and down, judging my wardrobe. I was wearing a black sequined dress with square shoulders that gave me a powerful silhouette – one of my mother's favorite pieces she'd had re-tailored to fit me – but I still felt under-dressed compared to these people. Most of them were staring at Danny – he was easily recognizable, after all, as the sometime owner of this place, but their look wasn't just about respect for the most important person in the room. The women, especially, were looking at him with unbridled desire in their eyes. I flushed. I was with the man widely regarded as the most desirable in London. Back home in LA, I was treated like a catch, an eligible bachelorette. But here, I knew what the others were thinking. *Is she good enough for him? Does she measure up?* I wanted to vanish into the middle of the floor.

But Danny refused to be daunted. He took my hand and squeezed it, hard, showing all the world that we were there *together* before he kissed my palm. "They're just wondering what a lout like me is doing with a gorgeous thing like you," he whispered. "They know me here – same as your clubs in LA. It's a small world, and people here get nervous when they have to look at something unfamiliar. You're fresh meat. But don't you worry..."

"Fresh meat?" I smiled grimly. "Is that what I am?"

He laughed. "As utterly gorgeous as you are, to these people you're easy prey. Just ignore them."

"The VIP section, Mr. Blue," one of the maître d's almost bowed as he directed us to a private waterside dock covered by a white canopy. Inside, people were reclining on pillows at long tables stocked with every brand of champagne imaginable. As we made our way to the dock, we were intercepted by a tall woman in a perfectly-tailored black dress, her auburn hair swept up in an Audrey Hepburn updo.

"Can it be?" her accent had only the tiniest trace of a Scottish lilt. "Is Danny Blue back in town?" She kissed him immediately on both cheeks, lingering – I noted – just a few moments too long when she embraced him. She assessed me in a matter of seconds, her shrewd eyes taking in my height, attractiveness, and fashion sense, before apparently deciding I wasn't even worth bothering about and turning to Danny. "How *have* you been? What have you been up to, darling? It's been positively ages!"

"Joanne," Danny smiled through gritted teeth. "Always a pleasure. I've been in California."

"Oh yes, working on that little degree of yours – so charming!"

"And I don't believe you've met Neve Knight. Lead singer of the band I played with out there. The Never Knights. We're touring over here now."

"Oh yes, the Never Knights..." Joanne's voice dripped with disdain. "That teen band from America. I think my little sister has one of their songs on her iPod."

I wished for the floor to open and swallow me up. Danny, however, refused to take the bait. "Just signed with RRR." Danny said proudly.

"Well," Joanne said, looking utterly disingenuous. "So *good* that you've moved on, darling." She gave me a look full of contempt. "After that horrible business with Peyton. Oh, you know, I really do miss her quite dreadfully sometimes. She was so beautiful – inside and out – we all loved her *so* much." She squeezed Danny's hand. "We often think of her and you." She turned to me. "I never encountered a happier couple than those two, *really.* So utterly in love. We all absolutely mourn that terrible tragedy that took her from us." She looked over our shoulders. "Oh, my, is that Claire and Louis back from the Riviera? I simply must hear about their cruise!" She squeezed Danny's hand. "I know you must still be mourning. You have my number – do ring me if you ever need to...grieve." She turned to me. "Good luck with that little band of yours, er – Ever?"

"Never."

"Yes, of course." She looked down her nose at me as she glided off.

When she was gone I breathed a sigh of relief. "What was *that*?" I asked Danny.

Danny put his arm around me. "*That* was someone you shouldn't let bother you. The Honorable Joanne Waldegrave. Minor aristocracy. And Peyton's best friend – of a sort. Didn't stop her trying to seduce me repeatedly while Peyton was alive. She and Peyton were at the same college back in Oxford. Didn't pay a whit of attention to Peyton when she was just a middle-class girl from the North, but the second her band made it big it was Peyton darling this and Peyton honey that..." He scowled. "She turned up at my place only a few days after Peyton died, seeking to "comfort me." It didn't work. Couldn't even respect her so-called friend's memory that long..." He wrapped an arm around my waist, pulling me close.

"She made me feel so small."

"Please don't listen to her," he said. "Don't let a horrid jealous woman like that annoy you. Some people are just insensitive, and Joanne has the sensitivity of a rock." He sighed. "After this, my father should be a breeze."

The second my eyes fell upon Clarence Blue, I knew exactly what he was. Looking just like an older version of his son, Clarence looked closer to Danny's age than to his sixty-something years. I could still see the muscles rippling beneath his exquisitely tailored blue shirt. Handsome, cocky, charming, and magnetic, Clarence had whatever mysterious *it* it was that made Danny so utterly irresistible. But while Danny's blue eyes had a certain softness, a certain still sad haunting beauty, Clarence's eyes were hard and cold. Painfully aware of their own power. Next to him sat a waif-like blonde barely out of her teens – Roni Taylor. Even without makeup, Roni was one of the most beautiful women I'd seen, easily four inches taller than me and probably still weighing at least ten pounds less. She picked sadly at a pile of lettuce arranged florally in the middle of her plate, her eyes only lighting up when she saw Danny approach. She was wearing an off-the-shoulder peach dress that highlighted her bony shoulders. I was intimidated by her and felt sorry for her at the same time. She was beautiful, terrifyingly so, but almost bird-like – like a bird, I thought, trapped in a cage. Eating forkfuls of plain lettuce.

"So, this is the girl you haven't shut up about!" Clarence's broad Yorkshire accent was a far cry from Danny's clipped tones, but the deep bass timbre in the voice was the same. "Let's have a look at her, shall we? Are you the girl that's been vexing our Danny?" He looked me over, his bright blue eyes watering slightly as he took in every inch of my flesh with an interest that seemed decidedly more than paternal. I shivered slightly as he took hold of my hand and kissed it with mock obeisance. "Danny's been spending a fair bit of time out in California – is that your doing, my girl?"

"Father..." Danny said in warning tones, looking thoroughly uncomfortable at the proceedings. "Neve's new here – let's make her feel welcome."

"Charmed," said Roni Taylor in a hollow voice, automatically stretching her hand out to me. She looked like a doll, I thought, every action, every gesture meticulously rehearsed. She was evidently as nervous as I was, trying to make a good impression. My pity for her increased. A girl of twenty-one married to a man three times her age, trying to fit in among the snobs and dandies of the Blue Water nightclub, among women like Joanne who would likely treat her with the same withering disdain. What was she doing with herself? Did she find any friends in a place like this – or only enemies?

"Roni, so good to see you." Danny's voice was curt, almost wary. I looked up in surprise at his tone of voice. Danny was normally so friendly; why did he sound so awkward around her?

Roni's blue eyes narrowed on Danny's face, and her expression said it all. The look of boredom and misery faded; in that moment her eyes lit up and sparkled. I saw a glimpse of the beautiful, happy young girl that I'd seen on the cover of so many magazines. "Danny!" she said. "I've missed you so!" She pulled him to her in a hug, a hug that he nervously tried to get out of reciprocating.

My stomach plummeted as I realized the truth. The real reason Danny was so nervous about me meeting his family. Roni's look wasn't the look of lust or desire I'd learned to get used to on the faces of so many groupies. Roni Taylor was quite obviously head over heels in love with her stepson.

# Chapter 8

Clarence Blue looked me up and down, his limpid blue eyes fixating on me. I shivered slightly as I felt him take it all in – the size of my hips, the curve of my waist, the precise shape of my breasts. Clarence Blue was, I knew, more than just a womanizer – he was the ultimate playboy, every girl's dream. Or at least – he had been, and his bank account balance more than made up for the difference between his looks now and the looks he sported back in the day. I was thoroughly unnerved by the way that Clarence patted my shoulder, hugging me tightly enough to feel my bra strap under the dress; the way he looked me in the eye, searchingly, as if to imply that he knew exactly what Danny and I were doing every night. It was Danny's turn to be embarrassed. At his father's actions, he flushed a vague shade of crimson, looking down and trying to avoid my gaze. Poor Danny, I thought as Clarence Blue's eyes seemed to close in around me, it's one thing having a dad who used to be a famous womanizer in the past. But Clarence apparently wasn't above hitting on his son's girlfriends in the present. Perhaps it made him feel young again; certainly, the cheeky flirtatious grin he shot me wouldn't have looked out of place on a boy of sixteen.

"Well, you certainly can't say she doesn't have Jessica Botano's looks," Clarence said with a smirk. "She's stunning, Danny. Well done." The way he turned to Danny, completely ignoring me or any say I might have in the matter, hit me to the core. I flushed red with embarrassment against myself.

"Thank you," I said stiffly. I couldn't risk being impolite now – as nervous as I felt, I knew the last thing I wanted to do was isolate Danny's parents. However unconventional this was, this was definitely a "meet the parents" moment. A chance to impress Danny, to show him that I was long-term girlfriend material. Just like Peyton was. *Peyton...* I caught a glimpse of Joanne on the barge, laughing and flirting. Was what she said about Danny true? Had he already had it – that one great love that makes all others seem meaningless by comparison? I swallowed hard and tried to ignore the sinking feeling in the pit of my stomach. Could I only be second best for Danny?

"She may be Jessica Botano's daughter," Danny shot out, taking my hand, "but her beauty is all her own. Neve's one of a kind, Dad." His voice took on a strange, child-like urgency. He wasn't just complimenting me, I noted – he was trying to *convince* his dad, to gain some measure of approval from the father who barely seemed to notice that Danny existed. "And don't forget her talent. I mean, really, Dad, Neve's one of the best song-writers I've ever worked with. You must have heard it on the radio – our first single. It's selling rather well, actually."

"Yes, yes, I must have done," Clarence said airily, in a voice that made it clear he'd probably never bothered to do it. "Roni tells me what to listen to – don't you, Roni? She's in charge of my social media." He guffawed.

Roni leaned across the table, reaching out to lightly touch Danny's hand. Her eyes were blue and enormous, full of emotion. "It's really a very good song," she said. "I always like to keep track of whatever Danny's involved in. If he decides what he really wants to do is form a band, then I support him every step of the way." She smiled at him, but her maternal words felt strange – even unsettling – coming from her lips. The way that Roni – clearly a couple of years younger than Danny – was affecting this parental role even as her eyes nakedly told the story of her longing for him bordered on the surreal. I felt thoroughly uncomfortable, although from the looks of it not nearly as uncomfortable as Danny. No sooner had she reached out to touch his hand than he visibly stiffened, shooting me an almost apologetic look. Against myself, I felt an instinctive stirring of jealousy. Was Danny genuinely uncomfortable with the way Roni Taylor – a woman so beautiful it made you want to stop whatever you were doing to paint a sculpture of her – looked at him, or was he just embarrassed about revealing her feelings for him in front of me or his father? I couldn't imagine any guy turning down a girl that looked like Roni, and my heart sank slowly. This whole family was decidedly more eccentric than my own.

"Yes, yes, well, well – we've all got our wild oats to sow, eh?" Clarence winked and nudged Danny in the ribs, looking at me with a decidedly emphatic stare. "But eventually we learn to grow up and do the right thing, isn't that right, Danny? I'm hoping once Danny finally gets this degree business out of the way we'll see some proper use out of him at Blue Enterprises."

"Dad..." Danny's voice was filled with warning. His father's words had evidently cut him to the core. Never before had I seen Danny look so small, so vulnerable. He looked almost like a schoolboy being chastised by a schoolmaster. So very young. So hurt. His father evidently had more than his fair share of power over him. No wonder Danny had been so reticent to let us meet – to let me see him in this vulnerable state.

"Oh, for goodness' sake, Danny – do be an adult. Fiddling around with footnotes. Strumming a few chords on a guitar? When I was your age I'd already earned the money to buy a derelict old building in Islington that later became the first Blue Grand by whatever means necessary. I shone shoes. I sold newspapers..."

"Of course," Danny muttered, "the whole rags-to-riches narrative only comes out when it suits you."

"You've got a role to play as the President of Blues Enterprises. I gave you that title a year ago and you've done nothing with it but have a shiny nameplate on an unused office..."

### Never Land (The Never Knights #2)

*Blues Enterprises?* I looked up in confusion. Danny had told me that he was minimally involved in his father's business. Being named as President of Blues Enterprises was more than just an honorary title. It meant that Danny had control of millions of dollars of company funds – whole bales of cash at his fingertips. Why had he never told me that? Danny was looking down shamefacedly.

"Had I realized this evening was going to be an ambush..." he was saying quietly.

"I realize that your thoughts were elsewhere because of the Peyton incident, and believe me, I gave you time to recover, but it's been a year."

"Dad!" Danny looked absolutely shocked and appalled. "The *incident*? Really? Is that what you call it – the *incident*? She's dead, Dad. Dead. A woman is dead – and if you can't bear to refer to her by name..."

Clarence seemed airily oblivious to his son's distress. "And this band you're in," he snorted. "At least when you were in with Peyton you seemed to take your music somewhat seriously. But this new band seems like a game of musical chairs. You're out, you're in, you're in, you're out. Not exactly the actions of a man dedicated to his craft – or to doing anything much more than appeasing his girlfriend, lovely though she may be."

I felt anger surging through me. In a few well-chosen words, Clarence had been able not merely to insult Danny, to embarrass us both about Danny's lingering feelings for Peyton, and to dismiss his son's ambitions and loves in a single breath, but he'd also insulted the band. His words were an insult to me, to Luc and Kyle and Steve and even Geoff, to everyone who had worked hard to make the band great, something to be proud of, something more than a vanity project for a couple of over-privileged Beverly Hills teenagers. At that moment I didn't care whether or not Clarence Blue liked me, or whether he *approved* of me as Danny's girlfriend, whatever that even meant. At that moment all I knew was that nobody, absolutely nobody, could get away with insulting the Never Knights in front of me.

"Mr. Blue," I began, my voice firm, but clear, "I do appreciate your kindness in inviting me here tonight, but if you for a second believe that the Never Knights is anything but a group of incredibly talented, incredibly hardworking people – Danny among them, I might and – I will have to forcibly refute you on that point. The chief scout of RRR, Richard Slayton, personally chose to sign us – he put his reputation on the line because he believed we had what it takes. And so do I." I stood. "It was nice meeting you both..."

For a moment, Clarence Blue looked at me agape, taken aback. Then, after one horrible silent moment, he broke out into shocked laughter. "Sit down, miss," he said. "You've got yourself a firecracker, haven't you, Danny? She's certainly a lively one." He had realized that his words had gone too far in front of me, and now he was turning on the charm to make up for it. I wasn't sure if I was relieved or appalled at his next word. "Perhaps you're right, Miss Knight, I did sound a tad dismissive. But you must realize the commitment Danny's taken on. About a year ago Danny agreed to do as I asked and take on a leadership role in Blue Enterprises. I'm anxious to retire, to take a break from the business end of things, and like all proud fathers I do want my son as my successor. After the...tragedy, I granted him an indefinite leave of absence. But it was never my intent that this leave of absence become permanent. If he wanted to do his work in North America for a while, finish this degree of his, so be it. But eventually I will need Danny here. To control things alongside me."

"It's a big honor," Roni Taylor chimed in nervously. "Clarence would never trust his company with just anyone."

"But we need Danny with us, too," I said, taking Danny's hand, daring to look his father in the eye.

"And I intend to be with the Never Knights as long as they need me," Danny said. He squeezed my hand, and I felt electric warmth seep through me.

"As long as you're able to assume your duties as President," Clarence looked askance at his soon. "That's the important part..."

"I will do that. But I'm not going to let Neve down, either." Danny turned my face towards his, kissing me passionately – defiantly, even. Out of the corner of my eye I could see Roni's face go waxy pale.

"No, of course not..." Roni said, her voice smooth as silk. "What a hero our Danny is. Still going about saving his damsels in distress – just like he always did..."

I was going to reply with a statement about how I most decidedly was *not* in distress, but perhaps fortunately

I was interrupted by the appearance of an enormous trolley of rich desserts.

"I didn't order anything..." I looked down at the piles of chocolate cake, confused.

"Dad took the liberty of ordering," said Danny. "He likes to surprise his guests with dessert first. It's his style – isn't it, Dad?"

"Of course..."

Conversation started to turn to more neutral topics – the weather, London's latest attractions – and for a few seconds I was able to join in the fun, for a few minutes this felt like a dinner at Luc's family home: a raucous, loving family dinner.

Then I looked down at our plates – piled high with strange desserts, Roni's plate entirely empty except for a single cranberry, her face straining as she tried not to cry, Danny's face bright red, and I realized it – this would never be a normal family...

# Chapter 9

The rest of the dinner went by quickly. As confused as I was by Danny's strange family dynamics – his eccentric father's strange power over his son, what seemed like Roni's obsession with the boy she could never have, I had to admit that on a personal level I was growing to like Clarence Blue. He could be cold, officious, and controlling – but he could also, I quickly learned, be witty, funny, and charming. He'd gotten his reputation as a successful womanizer for a reason – he was very good at becoming the center of the room, the most important person in any argument. Even I found I couldn't take my eyes off him. While I didn't find him handsome – his relationship to Danny made such an appraisal all too weird – I could certainly see that Danny's charisma was at least partially genetic. And Clarence seemed to have, at least, decided I wasn't too terrible an influence on his son. When we parted he hugged me tightly and kissed me on the cheek.

"Goodbye, Neve," he said. "I get the feeling I'll be seeing you again."

"Got to go," Danny said. "Lots of errands to run. Neve's last night off in London, after all. "Danny's hand on my shoulder made it clear that he wanted to get out of there as quickly as possible. He led me swiftly out of the restaurant and into his silver Aston Martin, driving me through the streets of London, along the Thames, before heading north through a warren of streets and into the funky, bohemian district of Camden, where colorful houses were painted with bright murals. He turned a corner and stopped in front of what looked like a luxury apartment block overlooking the Regent's Canal.

We were silent as I followed Danny into the lobby and up the elevator to the penthouse. When at last he had opened the door, revealing a sumptuous Art Deco apartment filled with gorgeous furniture from the 1920's and '30's, my mouth fell open. "This is your place?"

Danny silenced me with a kiss. His mouth was hungry, even desperate as his lips sought mine, as his tongue traced the corners of my mouth; his sweat mingled into mine – we were both so alive, so aflame, with the sheer force of our desire. He pushed me hard against the wall, and I could feel the movement in his groin against my own that meant he wanted me here; he wanted me now. "I've been thinking about doing this to you all evening. All during that ghastly dinner. All the while, under the eyes of those two, I wanted nothing more than to rip off all your clothes and make you scream with ecstasy. I kept picturing what you were wearing under that gorgeously short dress of yours – and wondering if you were wearing anything at all. Let's see..."

I moaned slightly as his fingers slid between my legs, testing his query.

"Yes, by the way," he whispered as he covered my neck in kisses. "It is my place. Or at least – as much mine as anything I have. I've tried to keep it my escape – the one place I can be independent from my father." He stopped, sighing. "I bought it when my trust money from my mother came in when I turned eighteen – one of the few things I have that my father never controlled."

I took in the place. It was the most stunning apartment I'd ever seen – meticulously decorated. Filled with old records, with rock and roll posters, with photographs. Photographs I didn't even have to ask about before I knew what they were – pictures of Danny playing music, a beautiful blonde girl on the microphone. A girl whose eyes made me at once intimidated and ashamed. The gone girl Danny couldn't get out of his head. Peyton.

Perhaps Danny sensed my discomfort, for he came up behind me, wrapping his arms around my waist. "Shh...Neve, come with me," he led me away from the photographs and into the bedroom, undressing me tenderly as he pushed me into a sitting position on the bed, crouching before me so that his mouth was on the same level on my hips. He leaned forward, his tongue warm and welcome against me, and soon I was screaming his name, my whole body shuddering and tensing over and over again.

But this time, when at last Danny had clambered into bed alongside me, his warm naked body feeling so good against my own, the pleasure seemed less important. As I felt him move within me, felt our bodies joined together, I felt something else take place. I felt *close* to Danny – and he close to me. This strange evening, this odd family dynamic – these were things that showed me a whole new side to Danny Blue. A crazy, insane world of privilege and wealth and expectation, the likes of which I could only dream. I thought being Keith Knight's daughter was weird, but in practice our family was just like any other traditional "nuclear" family – a loving, if slightly eccentric, father, a doting mother, the occasional argument, a firm belief in each other, a trust that we were family first and celebrities – if that – second. Not something I'd seen from Danny tonight. I wanted to comfort him, to take away his pain, to give him all that he lacked – to let him know that I had faith in him, that I trusted him, that with me he was Danny, first, and Clarence Blue's son, second. I told him with my body, devoting each muscle in my body to intensifying his pleasure, and when at last we came together, our cries melding into one another, I found that I had tears in my eyes – and he in his.

"I love you, Danny Blue," I whispered.

He moaned a contented moan, his eyes closed.

"I can't get enough of you," he replied, kissing me. His eyes opened wide, and within them I saw a look of decided mischief. "Close your eyes."

"What are you going to do to me?"

### Never Land (The Never Knights #2)

"You'll see," Danny said. I followed his directions, and a moment later I felt something cool and moist against my skin. The delicious aroma of chocolate wafted through the air; my skin began to tingle with a pleasurable warmth.

"Chocolate body oil from Le Body Gourmet," he said. "I had them send over a gift basket." He lowered his head between my breasts and ran his tongue down to my navel. I shuddered and cried aloud as he worked the oil in with his fingers, his deft touch bringing me to ecstasy once again. "I could lick you all day, Neve Knight."

"Danny," I laughed. "I thought we had errands to run." I smiled and moaned as he answered me with a flick of his tongue.

"We do," said Danny. "Only...this comes first."

"What errands are we running, anyway?"

"I wanted to take you to my office," Danny said, kissing my thighs. "And then back here."

"Why?"

"I have a gift for you," he said. "I had it shipped to my office so somebody could sign for it – knowing it'd arrive the same time in London as I did."

"So your office, huh? I guess you're President, after all."

Danny's smiled faded slightly. "I owe my father a lot. I'm his only child. And he's right – I did make a commitment to him..." His voice faltered. Did Danny mean what he was saying – or had his father convinced him of it?

"And Roni?" I asked. "You and her...you seem nervous around her."

"She's my new stepmom," he said. "It's weird – having her married to my dad. And not my mom."

"Is that all?" I asked, searching Danny's eyes for the answer.

He sighed. "No, that's not all," he said. "There's something you should know, Neve – something I should have told you. Something that's an enormous – enormous secret. Soon after Peyton died – too soon – I listened to the advice of some friends who thought the best way to get me out of my depression was to set me up with another pretty blonde, to pressure me into dating before I was ready. They set me up with Veronica Taylor."

My mouth dropped open. "You *dated* your stepmom?"

He flushed. "This was long before she met my father..." he said.

**Never Land (The Never Knights #2)**

"For how long?"

"It was a matter of weeks," he said. "It was complicated. I was still in a state of severe depression, and when I went back to America that summer to work on my doctorate, we were still together, but only on a very casual basis. Which was all I could give her. Well, two months later, I read the society pages and find out my dad's engaged yet again. To her. He didn't call to tell me himself – I think he wanted to shock me, the way he always does. Always likes to be the hero of the story."

"Did he know..."

"No," Danny said. "And she – and I – want to keep it that way. It's better like this. I perhaps once thought I had some...glimmer of feelings for her, but all that vanished when I realized she was more interested in the Blue name than in who I was."

"But the way she looks at you – she's definitely reliving your past history..."

"Well, that's where it can stay," said Danny sharply. "In the past. With everything else about us." He traced his fingers against my cheek. "I'm with you now, Neve," he said throatily. "That's what matters." He bent down and kissed me, before starting to lick me again, before our bodies tensed and were ready for passion once more...

# Chapter 10

We didn't make it to our errands that night, nor did we manage to head back out to pick up my mysterious present at the offices of Blue Enterprises. Instead we stayed in bed, still ecstatically re-discovering each other's bodies after a long period of absence. I had almost forgotten just how smooth his skin was, just how hard the muscles around his abdomen were. I had almost forgotten the beautiful look in his eyes just as his body tensed in complete and utter pleasure, and the way in which he shuddered when he came. But I learned all this anew, as we spent the whole evening and much of the next morning in bed, exploring one another, re-connecting.

Yet, despite my pleasure, I couldn't help but feel a strange sick sense of worry at the pit of my stomach. Although I held Danny here in my arms, feeling them wrap around his sweet-smelling, firm flesh, I knew that there was a part of him I could never reach. Danny's strange and eccentric family, his odd upbringing, the way his father had convinced him to be part of Blue Enterprises, Veronica's acknowledged feelings for him – there was so much of Danny's life that I couldn't be part of, couldn't really understand. Just like Peyton. Although we were in the bedroom, I could feel her eyes boring into me all the way from the living room; I could feel her presence in this apartment. Had she and Danny had sex here, too? Had she too whispered that she loved him, and this time – had he said it back? My heart sank slightly. Even after all this time, Danny had never told me that he loved me. Was I just kidding myself? I knew Danny desired me, that he wanted to be near me – but *love*? That was something I wasn't sure I knew if he felt, or could ever feel again. There was so much to Danny Blue I didn't know. Who was I – just an eighteen-year-old girl, in a strange city, among strange people? How could I measure up to the self-assured, poised Joannes and Roni Taylors of the world, let alone Peyton – whose beauty, whose kindness, whose goodness, was legendary? Would Danny ever feel the same way about me as he had done about her, or would I always be an inferior echo?

### Never Land (The Never Knights #2)

I sighed and tried to forget about my worries. I was lucky, after all, I tried to tell myself. I had the man I loved naked in my arms, his arms twining around mine. Our first single was selling fast; only last night we had played the O2 arena. But something was missing, something....

The next day, however, I hardly had much time to dwell on my worries about Danny. No sooner had dawn first crept through the window than we headed over to our rehearsal venue to jam together so that we could get Danny up to speed on the latest songs. Luckily, our set list was largely the same as it had been in LA – we'd only tweaked a few very minor chords and added a bridge to one of our songs, and to our relief we found that Danny transitioned very naturally back into the Never Knights. His fingers had lost none of their nimbleness during his month-long absence from the band, no sooner had he picked up a guitar than the whole instrument was shaking, music seeming to pour forth entirely naturally from the guitar, beautiful music that spoke to my very core. Tonight we were opening for the Yeah Yeah Yeahs in East London, at a new nightclub called The Acropolis that I had heard was one of the most popular – and trendy – venues in the entire city. My whole body tingled with excitement. At last the band would be performing the way it was supposed to be – with Danny Blue on lead guitars, his voice and mine melding together into a single powerful wall of sound.

And that night onstage, we were better than ever. The energy and the passion that had driven our O2 performance was nothing compared to the pure ecstasy I felt onstage that night. All I had to do was look over at Danny to be reminded of the intense pleasure he had made me feel, the way he made me feel so alive, so full of energy, so full of possibility – feelings that I channeled into my song, my voice wavering and bellowing in turn as the song grew first soft, then loud, first sad, then powerful. The audience was lapping it up – they were screaming and shouting and crowding ever-closer to the front row to get the most out of our performance. And Danny's guitar, I noted, was more powerful even than Geoff. While Geoff had plenty of raw, natural talent, Danny brought something else to the strings of his guitar, as his solos echoed off the walls of the room. Quick, expert technique – the result of many years' practice – combined with his natural instinctive sense for rock sound served to create solos that were not just support for the main melody but rather, like classical music sonatas or symphonies, pieces of genuine art in themselves.

When we finished the performance that night I was drenched in sweat, adrenaline running high. The aftermath felt, like it always did, like a dream, as we were hurried from the stage into another black-leather-paneled VIP area, champagne piled high for us to drink, gorgeous groupies waiting backstage for us. I was tempted to stay, to taste some of the most expensive-looking cocktails I'd ever seen, which were waiting for us on a table that seemed to be made entirely out of ice, but Danny came up behind me and put his arms around my waist, nuzzling my ear, suggesting he had other plans. "All that playing," he said, "it makes me realize just how talented you are. And talent, love, is very – very sexy. What do you say we go back to mine?"

I didn't even think about hesitating. Within moments I was in Danny's car, speeding through London to get to his Camden apartment, already aroused by the mere thought of Danny's fingers, Danny's body. No sooner had we gotten into the elevators of the building than we were kissing passionately, hungrily, our bodies fused together by desire. But when we arrived in the penthouse, Danny frowned, turning towards the bedroom.

"I didn't leave that light on..." he muttered, looking worried. "Do you mind waiting here for a second, Neve?"

I nodded as Danny tiptoed into the bedroom. I tensed up. Who could it be? A burglar – a crazed fan...I shuddered as I remembered John Flint...

But instead I heard a female voice. Drunk, unbalanced, but still seductive even as she slurred her words. I tiptoed closer to the door, hearing the sound of loud, powerful female sobs. When I got close enough to make out the source of the tears, my mouth fell open. It was Veronica Taylor.

"Please..." she was saying. "I've wanted this for so long." I peered through the crack in the door in shock. Roni was completely naked except for a peach satin negligee that left little of her slender frame to the imagination. "Danny, please." She leaned in and kissed him quickly – all over his cheeks, his neck, his shoulders, her hands making for his jeans zipper at the groin until his hand stopped her.

Rage and pain washed over me, blinding me with shock and fury. So – Roni still believed she had a claim on Danny? But did he...

### Never Land (The Never Knights #2)

"Roni..." Danny's voice was stiff, full of warning. "Please – you're drunk, you're tired, you need to go home."

"I'm not!" she protested. Tears were streaming down her cheeks. "I made the worst mistake of my life, Danny. I'm trapped. You have to help me. I loved you – the whole time. Only ever you. I loved you so much that when you left I was angry, jealous. I wanted to get back at you for going away. But I regret...I've made such a mistake."

"Roni, please..." Danny was saying, trying to push her away. But was that a look of desire – however involuntary – that I saw glint across his eye?

"Just once, I want to feel you inside me again," Roni was pleading. "It was good for you, wasn't it, Danny? How it used to be?"

I could see that Danny was struggling to push her away. As she wrapped her arms around him, pushing him on the bed and straddling him with her toned, tan legs, I wondered what he would have done if I weren't here. Would he have succumbed to her fragile beauty – her passion?

"Roni, for goodness' sake, you're my *stepmom* now? Isn't that enough of a no? You shouldn't be here."

"I don't care!" she cried. "Danny, it's you I love – not your father."

"Well, you married him!" Danny grew angry – so angry that I could not help wondering whether his righteousness belied deeper feelings. "You made your own bed, Roni, now lie in it. I've moved on – and you need to, too."

"I can't stop thinking about you, Danny," she moaned. "I can't stop loving you. Nobody else can make love to me the way you can..."

I closed my eyes, feeling the tears seep in. I couldn't stand this pain, this jealousy, a moment longer. At that moment I didn't care that Danny was pushing Roni away, that he didn't want her. All I knew was that the secrets of his past were welling up, that I couldn't deal with more ghosts, more problems between us. Measuring up to Peyton was one thing – but there were only so many women I could compete with in the hopes that one day Danny would love me, only me! Tears streaming down my face, I ran from the apartment and made my way to the lobby, hailing a cab back to my hotel.

# Chapter 11

When I arrived back at our hotel, my eyes still wet with tears, all I wanted was to hide – to run upstairs to my room and pull the covers over my head. But as I entered the hotel lobby, I stopped short. Luc was sitting alone, sipping a drink, his expression melancholy. I approached him, surprised. I couldn't believe Luc was alone tonight – not if the number of groupies I'd seen hanging off him was anything to go by.

"Hey Neve," Luc's whole face lit up when he saw me. "Come on over!"

"What, no groupies tonight, Luc?" I meant to sound light, merry. But clearly my pain spilled over into my words, and my voice became bitter, even angry.

But Luc remained cool. All he said was "I was never into groupies, Neve. You know that." He lowered his eyes. Then he looked back up into my own, taking in my splotchy, tear-stained face. "Oh, Neve – what's happened?"

"Nothing..." I sniffed, but it was clear that I was lying. Nobody was a good enough actress to explain away the mascara running in rivulets down my cheeks.

"I thought you and Danny went off after the show. Did something happen?" Luc looked worried. "Is everything OK? If he hurt you, I swear, Neve, I'll..." his voice trailed off.

"No, it's fine," I insisted, knowing that my protestations would be in vain. Luc and I had been friends forever, and he knew me far too well to let me get away with these lies.

"It's not fine, Neve," he said gently. "You've clearly been crying. Come here," he pulled me in for a tight, warm hug. A hug that spelled warmth, friendship – that made me feel so safe, so secure, so taken care of after the stress of the last few days. I burst into tears. "Whatever it is, Neve, you can tell me. I promise. You know that, don't you?"

"Yes," I sobbed.

"What happened?" Luc pulled back, his fingers gently brushing a tear from my eyes. "Oh Neve, Neve, Neve, I hate to see you hurt like this. Let's get out of here, go someplace quiet so we can talk, okay?"

### Never Land (The Never Knights #2)

I nodded and he took my hand and led me to the elevator. No sooner had we entered the elevator than I saw Danny burst into the lobby of the hotel building, his eyes wild, his expression full of pain.

"Neve!" he called out, rushing towards me. He was breathless – clearly he'd rushed over here. "Let me explain..." His eyes fell upon Luc's hand on mine and they widened with worry. But I was too angry, too frustrated to worry about his feelings just then.

"I don't want to talk right now," I said.

"Neve, believe me, I can explain everything."

"Danny, I'm tired," I said, hearing my voice grow cold and weary. "I just want to go to bed. I'll call you later, okay?"

Luc took a warning step forward as the elevator doors closed on Danny's stricken, anguished face. I couldn't think about that right now. All I could think about was my own pain as I collapsed into Luc's arms, sobbing.

When we got to my room, Luc sat me down on the sofa, his strong arms around me. It felt good to be sitting with Luc like this. He was always the one I could rely on, the one who had comforted me whenever I needed a friend. Sitting with Luc like this – it reminded me of when we were kids, when some schoolyard bullying or mean girl's taunt sent me into floods of tears.

I couldn't help but laugh. "Remember that time you found me at the gym? After Stacey Stanford made fun of my military jacket and told me that none of the girls in my grade would be friends with me?"

Luc laughed, too. "Yeah," he said. "You were sitting in the corner of the gym, wearing this huge satin jacket with military lapels – and those horrid girls had torn them off you..."

I imitated Stacey Stanford's high-pitched voice. "Someone has to teach you what's acceptable and what's not, Never Knight." I sighed. "I really loved that jacket, you know? Dad had it made for me to match one of his. I was so proud of that jacket – I wore it everywhere..."

"But we fixed it, remember? You and I?"

"And your mom," I added. Mrs. Alamo had whipped out her needle and thread and put my jacket together in a jiffy. But now, I felt, my heart sinking, my problems would be a lot harder to solve. I sighed.

"Mom loves you like a daughter, Neve," said Luc. "And if she saw you crying, you know what she'd do?"

### Never Land (The Never Knights #2)

"Force feed me some pasta until I felt better?"

"She'd say "*una bella ragazza* like you can't be sad. Show me the *stronzo* who made you cry and I'll show him how *la mamma* handles things!""

Sitting with Luc like this felt so comfortable, so natural. I almost instinctively began to pour out my heart to him. "It's awful," I started. "Danny's stepmom..." I stopped short, realizing how selfish I was being. I knew how Luc felt about me, and I knew how much talking about Danny would hurt him. "Never mind," I said. "I don't really want to talk about it."

"Danny's stepmom?" My heart sank as a brief flash of jealousy appeared on his face. "So you met his family?"

"They live in London now," I explained, "so..."

"So Danny's stepmom? What can be so bad about her? Doesn't want to share her boy?" He chuckled. But one sight of my stricken face made him frown. "No, really – is it that?"

I nodded.

"But not...in a gross way?"

I nodded again.

"Like...*that* way?"

"She's twenty-one," I said. "And a supermodel."

"And she..."

I found myself telling Luc everything, as he egged me on to hear more, reacting with just as much shock and disgust as I felt.

"I can't believe I'm saying this," Luc said, "Because after all, I do have a vested interest in the matter – but it sounds like this one genuinely isn't Danny's fault. He's not interested in this woman – and honestly, who would be? She sounds like a serious creep. And it sounds like he's been faithful to you...even if I do wish you and he weren't together, I have to admit it. If it's meant to be, this woman isn't going to get in your way."

I was overcome by relief and gratitude at Luc's words. I knew how hard it must be for him to act like this with me, like a true friend. I threw my arms around him. "Luc, you always seem to know what to say," I said.

Luc stiffened, his voice growing husky. "If only I did," he said, his voice wavering ever so slightly. "If so, I would have said a few things sooner..."

As I looked up at him, I suddenly became conscious of how close he was to me, of how near our bodies were to one another, entwined in a hug on his sofa. For a moment I wanted nothing more than to stay like this, wrapped in his arms, feeling like this. But I knew for both our sakes, I needed to keep my distance. I pulled away. "I should go to bed," I said.

"No, I should go..." said Luc. "You're clearly...having a bad day, and I should leave you alone to deal with this. But if you ever need a friend, you know, I'm right down the hall." He smiled softly as he went out.

Yet after he closed the door behind him, I didn't feel remotely relieved. I knew Luc's words about Danny were true, but I also knew they didn't tell the whole story. It seemed that every time Danny and I got closer, every time it seemed as if our relationship might have a hint of a chance, some new complication separated us. First Peyton – whose photographs were plastered all over his walls even now – then his father – and now Roni. Why did everything always have to be so messy? I thought of Luc – stalwart, steadfast Luc, who had offered me a pure and simple love, and whom I had rejected, because next to Danny Blue's mesmerizing eyes, everything else fell short. But were those eyes, was that beauty, was that incredible smile just going to get me hurt in the end?

A knock sounded at the door. My heart leaped. Was it Danny – come to explain? But as I opened the door, my jaw dropped in utter shock. Standing before me, dressed in an exquisite camel-colored trenchcoat that showed off her svelte figure, was Veronica Taylor herself. Before even waiting for an invitation she sauntered past me into the room.

"What are you doing here?" I said, feeling my face flush hot.

"I wanted to talk to you," announced Roni, sitting down on the sofa imperiously, as if she owned the place. *Which, I guess, she kind of does.* "To establish some limits. Clearly, you don't understand that Danny and I are very close."

She got my hackles up, but I refused to let her see me sweat. I smiled as sweetly as I could muster and said, "Well, I can only imagine. Losing a mother is so hard – I'm so glad he's able to see you as another maternal figure."

She grimaced. "You know that's not what I'm talking about. Danny's not just my stepson – that, like everything else in my marriage, is just a formality. Danny and I knew each other long before I married Clarence. We were very close, and I enjoyed it."

"Until you married his father," I added, my smile still plastered on my face.

"Clarence is a – charming man," she replied smoothly. "I was young. Naïve. And he exposed me to a world I could never have dreamed of..."

"...filled with money you could have never earned yourself."

Veronica shot me a faux-injured look. "It's not about his money, you silly girl. There's nothing wrong with being attracted to a man who is a good provider. Who knows what he wants and how to get it."

"A sugar daddy?" I asked, my voice scathing with disdain.

"Please, dear," said Roni. "You're so naïve, looking at things so simplistically. I care greatly for Clarence. But I love Danny. All of Clarence's worldly charm – with certain skills one simply cannot get from an older man. I've never experienced such power, such passion..."

Her words made me sick to my stomach. Hearing such filth come out of Veronica's mouth made me want to run to the bathroom and vomit all over one of the meticulous Blue Enterprises Jacuzzis.

"So, what do you want me to do about it?" I asked – pretending to be far braver than I felt.

Roni didn't hesitate. "To ensure that neither you – nor anybody else, for that matter – holds Danny back from his bright future. He has great things ahead of him. If he's not distracted. *I* have plans for Danny."

"And your plans are the same as your husband's?"

"Not exactly. I want Danny to take over Blue Enterprises, just as his father does. Only, I want to do it sooner...and I want him."

Her eyes sparkled maliciously, and in an instant I understood her plan. Get Danny the President position – along with the position's billions of pounds' worth of perks. Make him financially secure before seducing him and leaving Clarence, getting her hot boy toy and her husband's money in one fell swoop.

"You're married. You're married to his father, you sick..."

I never got to finish my sentence. Roni slapped me clear across the face, and my cheek smarted from the blow.

### Never Land (The Never Knights #2)

"Whatever you think you know or understand, believe me, you don't." Her doll-like face had vanished – this Veronica was cold, steely, and filled with malice. "I'm not interested in having some child telling me what I can and cannot do." She stepped close to me, getting into my face. "I'm sure you think you're somebody. But believe me – you're just like every other wannabe celebutante, the daughter of a washed-up rock star and a sagging swimsuit model. You have no idea who you're dealing with. And if you know what's good for you, you'll stay away from Danny. If I see you together again, believe me – there will be consequences. Ta!"

As she glided serenely out the door, I had to sit down to avoid fainting from sheer shock. What kind of crazy woman would believe that she could actually convince me to stop seeing Danny? The same woman who would turn up in a negligee at her stepson's apartment and beg him to take her back. I swallowed, hard. Roni wasn't just some calculating gold-digger – she was genuinely, earnestly in love with Danny. Obsessed even. And that made her not just threatening, but genuinely dangerous.

I shuddered. Life with Danny was getting more complicated by the second.

# Chapter 12

For at least ten minutes after Roni left the room, I stood still – unable to move. Shock had flooded through me. I was exhausted – worn out. What had just happened? My face still burned, my cheek stinging from where Veronica's hand had collided with my face. The sound of the slap still rang in my ears. I vaguely heard my cell phone ring, but it seemed like the sound was coming to me underwater – the ringtone a million miles away. I couldn't focus on the ringing of the phone; I couldn't focus on the frequent beeps on the intercom, telling me someone was trying to reach me. I couldn't focus on anything at all except for the enormity of what had just happened. I'd known that Danny's life was a strange one, that life as Clarence Blue's son would make anyone a little eccentric. But now it seemed that Danny's secrets were so much greater than anything I had ever known. I'd always thought my own life must seem bizarre to outsiders – our money, our fame, the way, at the height of my dad's fame, we snuck out through the back door with balaclavas over our faces to avoid the paparazzi whenever we went shopping – but at its core our family life had always been a traditional one. My dad had been kind, if sometimes stern; my mother had always been loving. She'd of course maintained her natural flirtatious personality even after marriage – I knew that she was flattered by the attention that, for example, Kyle paid her, and that she knew full well the extent of my friends' childhood crushes on her – but the idea of her ever cheating on my father, let alone with one of my friends, was utterly alien to me.

But this woman seemed to be bound by no laws – either of society or of morality. In her eyes I had seen a conviction in her love, in her future with Danny, that bordered on the utterly unhinged. I put my fingers to the place that Veronica had slapped, wincing as I felt the bruised flesh, slightly swollen. Did people even slap one another, anymore? I'd only ever seen such a catty action in the old Hollywood films my dad and I used to watch on AMC when neither of us could sleep – black and white films with women with bleached-blonde hair and dark lipstick who traded barbed witticisms and fell victim to melodrama. But it seemed that Roni, with her natural air for the overly dramatic, believed that people actually did those things in real life. I grimaced, recalling some tabloid gossip from a few months ago about how Roni Taylor had planned to make a transition from modeling to film. *Guess she's practicing for the part*, I thought, trying to cheer myself up. But ridiculous or not, the slap had hurt, and my whole face burned from where her long red fingernails had left tiny marks.

Still dazed, I walked across the room to the lavatory, soaking a washcloth with warm water and holding it to my face. A champagne bucket filled with ice still waited for me outside the room; I took some ice and wrapped it in the washcloth, wiping my face, wiping away the small traces of blood she'd left with her nails. I looked at myself in the mirror. I was an absolute wreck. My mascara had run down my cheeks from the crying; my eyes were red. I was sweaty, bruised, smeared – utterly beaten down. Was this the face that gorgeous, merciless Roni had seen when she walked through that door in her thousand-dollar camel-colored trenchcoat? I wasn't much of a threat to her right now, I thought bitterly. Even at my best I'd have to struggle to be noticed next to the gazelle-like Roni – and right now I hardly looked anything like my best.

I sighed. Was this what Danny saw? After he'd seen Roni in her silk negligee, her legs stretching for what seemed like miles, her hair like a nimbus around her face, golden and shining – would he still want me in this way? Messy, chaotic – still stained with tears?

Yet as I looked at myself in the mirror, my self-pity gave way to anger as I thought about precisely what Roni had done. *How dare she?* I couldn't believe her audacity – an audacity that surely bordered on madness. "How dare she?" I said again, aloud this time, at my reflection, letting the weight of her actions sink in. Coming over to *my* house, telling me to stay away from my own boyfriend – a boyfriend to whom, incidentally, she not only had no right, but indeed was *her own stepson.* The whole situation was so ridiculous, so utterly sick, that I wasn't sure whether to laugh, cry, or scream.

Yet more anger seeped through me – this time not at Roni but at Danny. Surely Danny must have known how crazy Roni was – even if he no longer had any feelings for her. Surely he must have known how she'd react to the sight of him with a new girlfriend. And instead he'd chosen to try to handle the situation on his own. He hadn't warned me, hadn't prepared me – had allowed me to walk straight into a trap, to be mocked and humiliated by Joanne Waldegrave and Roni Taylor and goodness knew who else – allowed me to be made a fool of by everyone in his crazy, debauched life.

*How stupid could you be?* I recriminated myself. I'd seen this happen a hundred times among the girls and boys I'd grown up with. Always dating "within the group" - other Beverly Hills celebrities – always surprised when somehow people who grew up among models and strippers and playboys and alcoholics turned out to be functionally incapable of holding down an adult relationship. It was just one of many reasons I'd never dated in high school. I hadn't wanted to get sucked down by the dysfunction of yet another celebrity family. And here I was, dating the biggest celebrity of them all, Clarence Blue's son.

*But you didn't know he was Clarence Blue's son when you fell for him.* He'd just seemed like a normal guy – a normal, gorgeous, mind-numbingly sexy, talented guy, to be sure, but not the scion of a family of psychopaths. And every step of the way, he'd withheld information. About his identity, about his family, about his past. Letting me get close to him, letting me fall for him, telling me he was "addicted" to me, making me want him – only to push me away when it mattered. The classic bad boy maneuver I'd been warned about from the time I was ten.

How had I been so stupid? At that moment, all I wanted was to never see Danny again – to go back to where everything was normal, everything was easy, to men like Luc who never let you down. *Luc...* I felt a pang as his face came to mind. Luc would never have sprung his crazy family on me. He would never have set me up to fail the way Danny had...

I opened the front door, anxious to find Luc, to talk out my rage. But to my surprise, standing  before me was Danny himself, a look of utter anguish on his face.

"Neve..." he whispered, reaching his hands out to me.

*Damn it.* Just looking at him, the way his piercing blue eyes met my own, the sad look in his eyes that made me want to comfort him – everything about him made me melt. My anger, my fury vanished. All I wanted was for him to hold me tight. He stepped towards me and I could smell his familiar intoxicating musk – the combination of sweat and aftershave that made him so irresistible to me. Even now, my body wanted his.

"What happened to you?" He reached out and touched the angry red welt at my cheek. "Neve, are you okay?"

I looked down, my cheeks flushing crimson. I was too angry, too ashamed to tell him about Roni – would he even believe me if I did?

"Was it Geoff?" Danny's face clouded with anger.

"No, not Geoff." I shook my head. "Why – he's gone, isn't he?"

"No, Neve," Danny's eyes darkened. "I wanted to tell you – I put some of my dad's security staff on him. He hasn't gone back to the US like we thought. He's still in London."

"In London? Why?"

"Who knows?" Danny shrugged. "He's not stupid enough to try anything on you again – but just having him in this city makes me nervous..."

"Drugs aren't known for making someone make rational decisions," I said icily. "No, it wasn't Geoff. It was

– well..." I gritted my teeth, not looking forward to this conversation. "It was your stepmom, Danny."

His eyes widened with shock. "What? *Roni*?" His disbelief at first made my heart sink. Would he be so convinced of Roni's innocence that he'd blame me for this feud?

"Yes, Roni," I snapped. "She came here to warn me off you. Told me you were hers alone, and to get lost."

"Oh, Neve," Danny sighed, reaching out to touch me on my unbruised side. "Neve, Neve, Neve, I'm so sorry. I knew she was bad, but I didn't think it'll be this bad..." He led me into the suite, sitting me down on the bed, holding my hand tightly. "I should have known – I should have warned you..." He felt my bruise. "Did she hit you?"

"A slap," I said.

"It'll heal," he said. "It doesn't look too bad...let's get some more ice on that."

"She was really aggressive, Danny..."

"Typical Roni," Danny smiled grimly. "When she wants something, she'll go all out to get it. Snaring my dad into marrying her – playing all of us like a fiddle..."

His words were tinged with faint respect, or at least awe, and I couldn't help but feel the familiar jealousy wash over me as I remembered the sultry look in Roni's eyes as she had pushed her lips against Danny's own...Even knowing how crazy she was, I couldn't help but feel insanely jealous of her, of the way she made me feel...

"She wants *you*, Danny," I whispered, holding onto his fingers, not wanting to let go.

"Well, she can't have me," Danny said. He moved in closer and kissed me – softly at first, and then harder, passionately, making me moan as he sucked on my bottom lip. "I want you, Neve. You're the only woman I want. I'm with you." He pulled back, looking deep into my eyes.

I couldn't bear this pain any longer, or this anger. I just wanted to forget. Forget Roni, forget Clarence Blue – I just wanted everything to go back to the way it was before. Pure and simple – easy, passionate sex. I leaned in and kissed him, wrapping my arms around him and pulling him into me.

"Don't worry," he was whispering into my neck. "Believe me, Neve – you have no reason to worry. I want you and only you. I won't let her hurt you – hurt us...I'll prove it to you. You're the only woman I want, and I want you so badly right now..." He kissed me deeply, slowly; I felt my whole body shake with longing. He whispered into my ear, tickling the lobes with his tongue. "Do you want me to go further, Neve? I won't unless you want me to!"

"Yes!" I almost shouted it. *Yes, I want you. To make me scream. To make me forget.*

He pulled me onto the bed, undressing me, filling me with longing, playing me like an instrument, my whole body responding to his every touch as he brought me to the brink and then over it, again and again, until I was soaked and stained with sweat – mine and his – the sheets tangled between us. We fell asleep in each other's arms, and when we woke Danny's face was so angelic, so peaceful, that I felt a deep sadness rise in my throat. How could he sleep so softly, so dreamlessly, when so much confusion and complication hung between us?

I stood up to get a drink of water and noticed that an envelope had been slid under the door. Room service? I bent over to pick up the paper.

No sooner had I read it than my hands began to shake, sending the paper tumbling to the floor.

*You have been warned. If you refuse to listen to my wishes, there will be consequences.* It was unsigned, but I knew all too well the source of the note. Had she been outside – listening – all night? Was she standing in wait, outside – as Danny and I had sought solace in one another, as we'd made love?

I felt sick to my stomach.

Veronica was even crazier than I'd thought.

# Chapter 13

I gasped aloud. I looked down at the floor, the note fluttering downwards. I felt sick, nauseous. The whole world around me seemed to spin and turn; I grew dizzy.

"Are you okay, Neve?" Danny's soft voice called from the bed. "Neve, darling, what happened?"

But I couldn't think. My mind was going white, then blank, then white again – utterly blocking out any thought but the fear and nausea that were seeping through me.

"Neve, talk to me..."

I reached out to the bed, putting a hand down to steady myself. "She's crazy," I whispered. "She's really crazy. I don't believe it."

"What are you talking about?" Danny clambered over to the end of the bed, taking me in his arms. "Who's crazy?"

"Roni," I said, my voice faltering. "Your 'she's not that big a threat.'"

"Roni?" Danny looked confused.

## Kailin Gow

I picked up the paper gingerly, as if it were a piece of hot coal, and showed it to him. "She slid this under our door last night," I said, my gorge rising. "While we were...you know. She came back and wanted me to see this."

Danny's eyes widened as he took the note from me and began to read it. "This is insane," he said at last when he had finished, his jaw dropping. "Are you sure this is from her – not an imposter? Or someone trying to mess with you?"

"Believe me, I'm sure," I said firmly. "After all, I've spoken to her. I know what she's like."

Danny gritted his teeth. "You're right," he said. "She is – absolutely mad. Completely unstable." He turned to me, pain in his eyes. "You'll be careful, right, Neve?" He pressed my hands to his lips. "Promise me you'll be careful, okay?" He sighed deeply. "I'll take care of Roni as best I can. I'll do what I have to do – even if it means telling my father what I know about her. But between her and Geoff..." He kissed me, holding me close. "Listen, whatever you do, *don't worry*. I'll take care of this for you. I'll keep you safe, believe me." He held me tight and close, kissing me passionately. He tasted sweet, slightly salty, his body still warm from our exertions of the night before. "Do you trust me?" His eyes grew wide, and within them I could see that signature soulful look that still had the power to make me melt. "Do you trust me, Neve?"

I only hesitated for a moment. "Of course I trust you," I said, reaching out and taking his hands into my own. "Do you trust *me?"*

"Of course I do," he said. "It's been so long since I trusted anyone the way I trust you. It's never been this way, not since..." his voice trailed off, and I felt a pang at the absence, at the presence of what he did not say, of *her* name.

"Let me show you how much I trust you," Danny whispered throatily, taking me into his arms. He covered my whole body with kisses – fervent, hurried kisses, each one faster and sharper than the next, as if to cover me completely, to drown me in the force of his passion. Every kiss seemed to say to me – *trust me. I care for you. I want only you.* Each kiss seemed to drive the tension, the fear out of my body. I took in his whole naked body, delirious with joy at his beauty. At his rippled muscles, his bare flesh. At the tattoo of a blue lion beneath his right breast that looked so perfect, so intoxicating, against his tanned flesh. I loved feeling his body against mine; I loved feeling him inside me. It meant that we were close, he and I – a closeness that managed to cancel out all the pain, all the worry, all the vicissitudes of the outside world. Roni could come between us – she could make me jealous with a simple toss of her beautiful doll-like head – but she could never come between us *here*, here where Danny's body seemed to meld into my own. I closed my eyes and moaned aloud as Danny's fingers found the place that always made me cry aloud for joy that made my body shiver in delirious waves of ecstasy.

It was only afterward when, showering together, washing away the sticky sweet smell of sex off our bodies, that I realized how tired and hungry I was. It was getting close to noon, and I hadn't eaten dinner last night. I hadn't eaten anything since before Roni had shown up to Danny's apartment – and my stomach gave a loud rumble. Danny grinned at me. "I think it's time I showed you one of this country's most innovative inventions. I refer, of course, to the classic English fry-up?"

## Never Land (The Never Knights #2)

I groaned. "All that grease – first thing in the morning?"

"I could take you to the bog-standard version. A cheap cafe with slightly dubious sausages. But I've got an idea that might appeal more to your Californian nature, love. There's a lovely little brunch place in South Kensington that does rather more...elaborate fry-ups. Game sausages, free range eggs, ethically sourced food – the works. Does that sound a bit more your style?"

I smiled. "I could use some free range eggs right about now."

"Come on..." Danny took my hand, and before I knew it we were driving through the picturesque streets of South Kensington, a posh district with a decidedly European atmosphere. Little cafes and boutiques dotted the small, historic streets; the smell of baking bread wafted from a French patisserie on the corner. Danny led me into one cafe on a street corner, greeting the waitresses – who all knew him, I noted – and ordering us two enormous platters of breakfast.

Yet no sooner had I put a steaming forkful of eggs into my mouth than we were interrupted by a low, almost sad voice.

"Danny?" It was the voice of a woman in her mid-fifties, an elegantly-kept woman with a pale blonde bob and a meticulously tailored coat. The wrinkles on her face did little to mar her beauty – she had the kind, warm, sophisticated look of a woman who has aged into her years with grace and wisdom. Her face was familiar – strangely familiar, I thought, but I could not place it. Next to her stood a stunningly handsome blonde man, perhaps a few years older than me, with a boyish smile that seemed to fade on his lips when he saw Danny. He sighed quietly, approaching warily.

"Oh, Danny, how have you been?" The woman reached out and hugged Danny – tightly, to my surprise – so tightly that it seemed to make even Danny uncomfortable. "I heard you went away..." Her voice wavered.

"Yeah," Danny looked down. He looked embarrassed, shy – not like his usual confident self. "I'm so sorry – I meant to keep in touch, I really did."

"Of course," the man said, his voice slightly curt.

"We have missed you, Danny," said the woman. "Please do give us a ring sometime if you're ever in

London. It would be our pleasure to see you again, wouldn't it, Pete?"

"Sure," said the man, in a voice that made it clear that he didn't mean it.

"Whenever you need anything, Danny – you've always got a home with us." The woman squeezed Danny's hand, smiling a smile that – I noticed with curiosity, seemed marred by tears. Then the two of them hurried out of the cafe, leaving me alone with Danny. The one called Pete looked back at me, a strange and inscrutable expression on his face. Not the hostile look of contempt I'd been used to getting from Danny's "set" here in London – but certainly not friendliness either. He looked curious – intrigued, even. But Danny had made no effort to introduce me.

"What was that?" I asked him.

Danny looked uncomfortable. "That," he said slowly, "is Peyton's mother. And her kid brother, Pete." He swallowed. "Well, not really a kid anymore, is he? They moved down to London after...after Peyton's father died. Poor woman. Losing a daughter and a husband in five years."

I swallowed hard, flushing pink. No matter where I went, it seemed, I couldn't get away from Peyton's shadow. Her perfection. Her death.

"I'd tried to stay in touch with them, you know, after the accident. To make sure they had whatever they needed." He looked down at his plate. "But when I left for America again, we lost touch. It was too painful. I'd been one of the family – like a son to them. Pete and I were like brothers. But after Peyton's death...." He sighed deeply. "Her mother forgives me. Perhaps she shouldn't – but she does. But Pete...he thinks I'm responsible for killing his sister." His eyes grew dark. "And perhaps I am, Neve..."

"Don't say that." I too had grown pale. Seeing the effect Peyton had on Danny, even in death, was enough to undo all the confidence I had regained in Danny's arms this morning. Enough to make me wonder what I was doing with this man who – crazy stepmother or not – was clearly in love with a ghost. I tried to swallow down the tears along with the worry.

But Danny noticed my discomfort. Taking my hands and squeezing them across the table, he raised them to his lips. "Come on, cheer up," he said. "I've got a present for you, remember? We've got to head on over to Blues Enterprises – it's waiting for you there..."

I slipped my hand in his. "Okay," I said brightly. But deep down, I couldn't ignore the pain in my heart. I kept thinking of the look on Pete's face, of the tears in his mother's eyes, of the shame and guilt on Danny's face.

But even now, all it took was a squeeze of his hand, and I was Danny's again. I bit my lip. I was an animal, caught in a trap of my own making. I couldn't stay – nor could I go.

*You fool, Neve.* I whispered to myself. *Why did you ever fall in love?*

# Chapter 14

After brunch, Danny led me to his father's offices at Blue Enterprises. The office building – an enormous chrome-plated skyscraper that stretched almost into the clouds – was one of the most impressive, intimidating-looking buildings I'd ever seen. The lobby was constructed out of gilt and marble, with plush red velvet chairs and Persian carpets; the elevator was made out of clear glass, so that the comings and goings of the various workers were completely visible. This was more than just your average office building – it was Clarence Blue's dreamscape, as decadent and over-the-top and whimsical as the man itself. No sooner had we walked in through the front door of the lobby, the doorman waving us over to the special VIP elevator, than I saw Danny noticeably stiffen. This whole building seemed to have a cloying effect on him – the power of his father looming over him from however many miles away. He seemed paler, less healthy – as if the building were draining him of all of his life force, all of his strength.

"Come on," said Danny hoarsely. He didn't look like he wanted to talk too much about the way he'd suddenly blanched, as if in fear. He smiled and took my hand, evidently putting on a brave face. My heart went out to him. How I wanted to comfort him, to make him smile, to kiss the color back into his cheeks. "I have to show you something."

In a corner of Danny's elegant office lay an enormous wrapped box – one that, I noted as I stepped closer, my heart beating faster and faster with excitement – had a distinctive hourglass shape I knew all too well. I couldn't help the excitement in my eyes as I expectantly looked over at Danny.

"Go on then, love," Danny said grinning. "Open it."

I tore off the wrapping paper, guessing what it was; as I lifted the box, my hopes were confirmed.

"A guitar," I breathed, picking up the gorgeous instrument from its case. I stroked the frets, running my fingers up and down the strings. It was the most beautiful guitar I'd ever seen. As I felt its weight in my hand, I knew that this guitar was more than just attractive – it was a great instrument, hand-made, specifically crafted to my hands.

"I had them custom make it," Danny explained, turning red almost sheepishly. "Just for you. Sized from my memory exactly to fit your body and hands like a glove. But the design by the strings, here..." He pointed to the blue lion sketched at the corner of the guitar. "That I painted myself."

I smiled with recognition. The tiny blue lion matched almost exactly the tattoo I had recognized on Danny's chest. My heart swelled with happiness as my cheeks flushed pink. Danny wasn't just giving me a guitar – he was giving me a part of himself, an image that he wore so close to his own heart every day. I held the guitar in my hands, cradling it close as if it were a child, all the way back to Danny's place, overwhelmed by his gesture. Danny seemed embarrassed by his own emotion; he kept smiling and blushing and looking down as he saw how much I loved the new guitar, watching me play with the strings, unable to wait until we got back home to plug it into the amplifier and see how it sounded.

### Never Land (The Never Knights #2)

Could Danny be trying to tell me something? After all this time, was he finally ready to let me know that he was ready to move on – past Peyton, past Roni – past all the stress, and towards me instead? Was I finally the girl that mattered to him – not just as a present fling but as the girl he could think about making a future with?

The second we crossed the front door and I had laid the guitar down gingerly, even tenderly, I found myself in his arms once again, pressing my lips against his, hungrily trying to make him understand how much this gift had meant to me. "Let me thank you properly," I moaned aloud, pushing him into the bedroom, my body aflame with longing. As we entered his bedroom, as he pushed me down onto the bed, I remembered involuntarily the events of less than twenty-four hours earlier. How I'd stood in the front hall watching Roni's near-naked body writhe with desire through a crack in the door, watching her try to seduce the man I loved. I recalled that feeling of powerlessness, of rage, and this in turn filled me with a new and more fervent desire: to prove to Danny once and for all that my body – my legs and hips and thighs and breasts – were more beautiful, more mesmerizing, more alluring than hers. I climbed on top of him, straddling him with my thighs, pressing his hands against my breasts, arching my back and rearing up with pleasure.

"Neve..." said Danny, his voice half-admiring, playful. "What's gotten into you, tonight?"

I had to show him what I could offer – what I could give. Show him the woman he could love – if only he would let me in, let me closer, show me the side of himself I didn't yet understand, the mystery behind his pain.

When we made love it was powerful, electric. My whole body felt shattered by the pure and primal force of him. I had to erase every last memory of this place as it had been last night when Veronica had polluted it, every memory that separated me from Danny's arms.

After we had finished I lay in his arms, tracing my fingers across his magnificent torso, my eyes lingering on the blue lion. What did it mean? A symbol of love – a connection with me? I almost hated to ask – to ask meant to imply that other, more dangerous question. *Did Peyton get one, too?* I bit my lip, but I needed to know. I couldn't bear the questions, the secrecy.

"Danny..."

"Yes, love?"

### Never Land (The Never Knights #2)

"Your tattoo. It's the same as the one on my guitar."

"Yes – yes, it is..." He inhaled sharply.

"What does it mean? Where did you get it?" *With Peyton?*

There was a long pause, and my stomach dropped. Had I gone too far – asked too much of him? I flushed, flustered. "I mean, you don't have to tell me if you don't want to. If it's private or something."

"No, it's not private," said Danny. "No – it had to do with...memorializing someone who meant a great deal to me. Someone I miss every day."

*Peyton.* My heart sank. There was no escaping her – not in this bed, not here, not ever.

"My mother."

"Your mother?" I sat up in surprise.

"Years after she died..." Danny twisted his mouth, pain spreading over his face. "Car accident up in skiing resort in the Alps. Snow and ice on the track. Just my luck, isn't it? I should never get in a car with another woman I love again..." His laugh was black and bitter. "When I was little, Neve, my mother used to read me stories. All the wonderful English schoolboy stories – King Arthur and Robin Hood and brave Lancelot and the other knights of the Round Table and all the ones you get in storybooks. Princes and princesses – fearsome dragons and chivalrous knights. She used to call me her little lion-heart – Daniel the Lion-Hearted. She would tell stories about this brave Sir Daniel, most noble knight in all the land." His lip quivered slightly, and my heart – my whole body – ached for him. I wanted to comfort him, to wipe his tears away.

"She was what I always pictured a princess looking like. Beautiful, to be sure – but more than that. With a kind light radiating through her eyes, a certain inner serenity that made you feel as if there was nothing in the world that could cause her love to waver or become uncertain, even for a moment. A light I haven't seen since – except, perhaps, with you. Perhaps when we first met, that's what I saw in you. Another woman – a princess. That dress you wore the first time you stayed over at my beach house, it took my breath away, reminded me of a storybook princess." He shook his head. "No, you were something else. Something different. In your fire, in your passion for life, I saw the person my mother always dreamed I could be; the person I have long-feared I could never be. The knight – lion-hearted. Strong. Perhaps that's why I was drawn to you from the start." He chuckled. "Not because of what my body sought in yours – but something stronger, deeper. A need we had to explore lest it consume us." I could hardly breathe. I closed my eyes as Danny leaned in to kiss me, my heart beating so fast I thought it would burst.

"So it wasn't just the sex?" I smiled, teasing him slightly.

"Not just the sex," he leaned in and bit my lip lightly. "Though it helped. My little lioness..." He stopped and sighed. "But you see – I was never that knight. Never that man she dreamed I would be. At least not according to my father."

"What do you mean?"

"I look like my mother – everyone says that. I reminded him of her – perhaps. Of the woman he had lost. My mother wasn't like his later wives – young women he exploits and manipulates into marrying him, humiliating them in the tabloids, never measuring up to my mother. He loved her with a love that was pure and strong. She loved him before he was ever rich, ever famous – and he loved her. Head over heels. I always thought they were the ideal couple when I was growing up – but all that changed..."

"When your mother died?"

Danny blanched. "Yes," he said slowly. "When she died. We were coming back from the ski slopes near Mont Blanc, driving back to the chalet we'd rented. I was being a little brat – I was tired and hungry and whining that I wanted to get dinner before we headed back home." He closed his eyes, a look of utter anguish covering his face. "My father refused – he said he wanted to get back before it got dark, the roads were too dangerous. I was bawling and screaming like a little idiot, and my mother took pity on me and asked him to stop. She said I wouldn't be a little boy much longer and why not spoil me while we still could. My father refused – said it was time I grew up and learned to be a man and that I couldn't have everything I wanted. The two of them started to argue – on those icy roads – they were fighting and shouting and yelling as they almost never fought – so distracted they didn't see the oncoming car..."

Tears were falling from his eyes. "We plowed into the truck sideways. My mother was in the back seat with me – she ducked to cover me and that was the only reason I survived. Because the shards of glass that exploded into the car hit her first, not me. My father was knocked unconscious – my mother died on the spot. Their last words to one another had been an argument."

I felt my hands grew wet – and soon I realized why. I too was crying, my tears dropping with his. How great a burden Danny carried – feeling responsible for not one but two deaths in his life...my heart went out to him. I reached out for his hand, wanting to press it to my lips.

"He's never looked at me the same way since, you know," said Danny. "He's never been the same. But I know the truth – behind the playboy facade, the pressure, the lies. They were so close – until I came along. Until a whiny brat caused the argument that took my mother's life, that took her from it. He can't look at me without seeing that tantrum that cost him the woman he loved...the little boy I used to be – my mother's killer..."

"That can't be," I said. "Nobody could blame you for that – you were only a little boy. And your mother gave up her life for you – nobody can blame you for that...that's what mothers do for their children."

"He sent me away to boarding school when I was eight. I spent holidays with relatives – a few awkward dinners with him now and then. Barely saw him until I graduated Oxford – when he decided to take an interest in

me, in my life. But now, even now, we're like strangers."
He sighed deeply. "But Neve, he's the only family I've got.
The only one with any memories of my mother."

I took him into my arms, wrapping my body around
his, letting him cry, his tears hot upon my breast. I felt
myself cry with him, my body dissolving into sobs – our
pain melding together.

"I've never told anybody that before," Danny
whispered. "No one except you."

I stroked his hair, kissing his forehead, unable to
speak. Danny's pain – the tragedy that I had first noticed
when I looked into those dark Byronic eyes – was
bottomless: a story I had only just begun to understand. No
wonder why he couldn't have anyone get close to him. He
was afraid he'd end up killing them.

I looked into his baby blue eyes with his dark lashes
wet from my tears and his mixed. My heart squeezed in my
ribcage so tightly I could hardly breathe. I loved him so
much. My Danny Blue.

But could I save him?

# Chapter 15

The next few days were a whirlwind of gigs. We extended our stay in England. Every single night we had something going on – small performances in intimate cabaret settings, a couple of opening acts at larger arenas. I hardly had time to worry about my relationship with Danny, let alone my feelings for the rest of the band members. I barely even had time to breathe. Life on tour was exhilarating, to be sure, but it was also exhausting. Danny and I hardly had time to see one another; before I knew it, I was getting up at five or six in the morning to practice and rehearsing all the way through showtime. Of course, I couldn't really complain. No matter how tired I thought I was, no matter how much it felt as if my whole body were about to collapse, there was something about striding out onstage in the perfectly fitting couture costumes Cassie had ensured were delivered straight to my hotel room that made me feel alive again, full of energy. All at once – it seemed – we'd made it. We were living the dream. The five of us were pictured on the cover of *Rolling*

*Stone* - looking every inch the rock stars we'd wanted to be. We had personal shoppers to dress us; we had paparazzi following our every move. I'd watched my dad go through this when I was younger – I was used to being around fame. But somehow it was different when it was me, when it was all of us in the limelight. I got used to the expertly tailored clothes that Cassie lay out before me – to the cocktails and the bottles of champagne and above all things to the applause that greeted us all every time we walked onstage. It was easy to start to take these things for granted, to see them as just automatic perks of the job. But for me, each VIP Lounge entrance, each free bottle of Veuve Cliquot, was more than just a luxurious benefit. It was a reminder that someone, somewhere, thought we were important enough to care about, important enough to support. Someone out there believed in us.

On our last night in London, we had a commitment that made all our hair stand on end. We were invited to the exclusive launch party of Blue Enterprises' newest venture – a cruise line. To celebrate, Clarence Blue had chartered a small boat on the Thames, stocking it with expensive liquor and kitting it out with a dance floor and some of the hottest

DJs in town – and he'd invited every A-List celebrity in the UK to boot. Kyle, Luc, and Steve were ecstatic – after all, they had no way of knowing that Danny was Clarence Blue's son – Danny had done everything possible to keep that particular bit of information quiet. But I was less excited. Just the thought of entering a room with Roni Taylor, let alone Danny's father, was enough to make me feel nauseous. But there was no way I could get out of going without explaining to Cassandra Curry the reason why, and Cassandra was in no mood to let me off easy.

"Everyone who's anyone will be there," she said sharply. "If you want to be a rock star, you have to play the part. It's not just about the music, sweetie. You've got to network. You've got to know the right people – and impress them. RRR has a close relationship with Blue Enterprises – and we want to keep it that way."

I had no choice but to go. Although I dreaded running into more painfully snooty society types – I was no more eager about running into Joanne Waldegrave than I was about running into Roni – I knew that if I was going to be trapped on a boat with them for several hours, I'd at least have to make sure I gave them no leverage to mock me. I wore a scandalously short green cocktail dress that played up the color of my eyes, making sure every inch of my tanned skin was shown off to perfection, thinking grimly that for all her beauty, Roni Taylor was as pale and pasty as a porcelain doll. I put on my makeup carefully, adding a distinctively gothic edge to my eyeliner, determined that I wouldn't let anyone – no matter how perfectly coiffed – see me at anything but my best. Not that I had to worry – Cassie wouldn't have let me out of the hotel if I hadn't been. She fussed over us as if we were small children who needed to be led, supervising every moment in the preparation process as if it were a rehearsal for a performance.

"Don't worry," Danny said. "I'll make it clear to Roni that her little games, her insanity hasn't gotten to me. I'm proud to show up with a girl as stunning as you on my arm, and I want the world to know it."

As we boarded the yacht, the five of us linking arms as we headed down the red carpet, paparazzi flashing cameras in our faces, I felt a curious sense of relief. We hadn't spent much time as a band together offstage – I'd been going off alone with Danny, and I got the distinct sense that both Kyle and Luc were actively avoiding me to stave off the awkwardness that had gotten worse now that Danny was back in the band. It felt good to be together again – a team, a unity. Together we were brilliant, powerful. Unstoppable. When we were like this I felt safe, secure. Like not even Roni Taylor could touch me. Certainly, the feeling of Danny taking my arm, kissing my hand, touching me in public only contributed to my sense of confidence. He cared for me – he wanted me – and he wanted the world to know that we were together.

It was only when I felt the watchful eye of Luc or Kyle on me that I grew anxious and flushed. It was one thing to avoid being romantic with Danny on-set or in the rehearsal room – but here? Were we here on business or pleasure?

Danny, for his part, was trying to do a bit of both. As the lead guitarist of the Never Knights, he was a celebrity guest, here to enjoy the booze and mug a bit for the paparazzi. But as the President of Blues Enterprises, he was here on business, and every now and then he left my side to talk to potential investors and make valuable business contacts.

As he went to chat to the owner of a Paris hotel about potential branding opportunities, I headed over to the deck, watching the full moon above me. I thought back to the last time I'd seen a moon as big and beautiful as this – after our performance almost two months ago, the night Danny and I had first consummated our feelings for each other. The night that everything changed. I sighed, thinking back to Danny's lips on mine...

"You can't ask for a more beautiful picture than that," said a deep, rich male voice behind me. I nearly jumped with surprise as I turned to find a familiar, handsome face. It was Peter – Peyton's brother – striding towards me in a casual but confident manner that gave him the bearing of a ship's captain. He smiled. "We met before," he said, as if I needed him to jog my memory. "I'm Peter Collins – we ran into you at Chez Montparnasse in South Ken. I'm – ah – a friend of Danny's"

"Yes, I remember," I said. I felt a strange sense of shame as I reached out to shake Peter's hand. Who was I to shake the hand of Peyton's brother, to remind him of the sister who no longer stood at Danny's side? But Pete was staring at me with a strange smile – not hostile at all, but rather radiating warmth.

"Any friend of Danny's is a friend of mine," I said.

### Never Land (The Never Knights #2)

"And what brings you here tonight?"

"Not quite sure, actually," Pete said, blushing slightly. "We received an invitation out of the blue – well, literally, I suppose. From the Blue family."

"You know them well?"

"Sort of..." Peter looked uncomfortable. "We've met, and all. Through Danny."

I tried not to think about what his words meant. That Peyton and Danny were serious enough for her to introduce Peter to Danny's father – and to another stepmother, since vanished, no doubt, into tabloid magazine obscurity. Peter was doing well, I thought – despite the elephant in the room. The sister I could never be. He was charming, polite, unfailingly friendly.

"So, Neve Knight," Pete said. "I must confess I'm a fan. I enjoy indie music – how does it feel, then, to be the next great band to hit the radio waves?"

I laughed. "You sound like a radio show host."

He blushed again. "For a reason," he said. "I do host a late-night radio show out in East London. But it's not a profession. More like a hobby, really. In the real world, I'm just a boring old architect."

"Nothing boring about architecture."

"It's not quite as sexy as punk rock," Pete said. "I thought I'd recognized you in South Ken – didn't realize you were *the* Neve Knight, though. You looked different without the punk stage makeup. Beautiful either way, of course," he added, embarrassed. "But I'd recognize your voice anywhere. I saw your profile in *Rolling Stone.*"

It was my turn to blush. "You mean the "Hello, I'm Keith Knight's Kid" piece?" I still hadn't gotten over the awkwardness of that one.

"More like the 'Hello, I'm Keith Knight's Kid – and I've still got a style of my own to show you,'" he said. "More Nancy Sinatra than..."

"Zowie Bowie?"

"Precisely." He grinned. "It certainly piqued my interest – and that of my colleagues." His slow, soft smile put me at ease as he put his hands against mine on the railing. It was a relief to talk to one person in this strange city who wasn't out to get me – even if he was someone who by all rights should resent me. Should resent that I was here, instead of *her.*

"I'm flattered," I said. "Didn't think the interview would be taken so well."

### Never Land (The Never Knights #2)

"Well, it certainly was," Peter said.

"So, Peter," I said, trying to change the subject so he'd avoid seeing my pink, embarrassed cheeks. "Tell me. I don't know a lot of Danny's friends. What was he like, growing up?"

Pete blanched slightly. "I didn't know him until he was a student at uni," he said. "He – uh – he used to date my sister, actually. He was nice, I suppose. Charming. Definitely had his demons – but you know all those posh boarding school types always have that sort of thing. Certainly, Peyton found him attractive..."

I winced slightly, feeling a tinge of guilt at having directed the conversation this way, having brought up Peyton's name.

"She died this time last year," he added.

"I know. I'm sorry..."

"No wonder you looked so awkward," Pete couldn't help but smile softly. "Bless you – you must have felt horrid, meeting us that day in South Ken. Please, don't feel..." He sighed. "I miss her every day. We all do. But...she wouldn't have wanted any of us to be unhappy, or to not move on. And it's not *you* who..." his voice trailed off. "I have to move on, you see. To be strong. For Mother, as much as for myself."

"He still misses her too, you know," I said to him. "Danny."

"Yes, well, *Danny...*" Pete grimaced. Evidently there were still some hard feelings there. "He's a tough nut to crack. Wouldn't have told me if he did. Then again, not sure he'll ever look me in the face again, after he..." he stopped himself. "There I go," he said. "Letting down all my countrymen. We're meant to have a stiff upper lip, aren't we? And here I go blabbing all my feelings to a perfect stranger."

"It's okay," I said. "I'm American – we all do that."

We both laughed.

"So Pete – why did you come all the way out here just to talk to me?"

"What can I say – I'm a fan? And I wasn't sure, at first, if you were Danny's friend – or something more...?" He stared at me intently, but before I could respond, Danny strode over to us, taking my arm.

"There you are, I've been looking all over for you!" He saw Peter and his smile vanished. "Oh, hello. Good to see you, you know, out and about."

### Never Land (The Never Knights #2)

"Indeed," Peter grew stiff, almost formal. "Enjoying a chat with Never here. Must say – she's got a rather odd habit of bringing you up the whole time we were talking. Odd, given that I wanted to know all about *her*. I know enough about you." His humor was dry and light, but beneath his wry smile I saw real pain.

"Always the young peacock, aren't you, Pete, trying to impress the ladies?"

"I learned from the best," said Peter. He was trying his best to joke with Danny, to engage with him in friendly banter, but I could see that the mere sight of Danny hurt him.

"Has this fellow been trying to impress you?" Danny turned to me.

"Not trying, succeeding," I said, trying to lighten the mood. "He's been very nice. What can I say? You Brits are all so charming."

"Not all of us," said Danny, shooting Peter a warning look. "Don't go sniffing round my girl, yeah, mate?"

"Your girl?" Pete looked me up and down. "So it's true, then." He sighed. "Well, if you were going to replace her, I'm glad it was with someone worth it."

His words stung. I knew he meant them kindly – but the truth of them was clear. Peyton's replacement. That's who I was, even now. And that's who I'd always be.

# Chapter 16

At that moment, all I wanted to do was get away. Get away from Danny, from Pete. From anyone who had ever seen or known or loved Peyton. Go back to the people who just knew me as me, for me, who didn't see in me only a missing and imperfect version of *her*. I wanted to go to Kyle, Luc, to Steve. To my friends – people who never compared me to anybody. Who saw only the girl I was, not the girl they wanted me to be.

"I'll let you two catch up," I said quickly, before walking away as quickly as I could, catching a glimpse of Danny's confused, sorrowful look as I turned. I made my way back to the main ballroom, where I could see Steve – completely plastered from the looks of it – dancing like some sort of maniac in the center of the room, surrounded by a bevy of gorgeous models. Kyle, meanwhile, was sitting alone at the bar, a look of strange sorrow across his face.

As I headed over to Kyle, a hand stopped me. It was

Cassie. "I've been told to round up the troops," she said shortly, "Can you nab Kyle for me? Slayton says there's something big happening tonight, some announcement they're making. He's not sure what it is – apparently it's all very hush-hush – but he says it's something big. The Blues want everyone to gather into the main ballroom. I'll get the others..."

I nodded. "Of course," I said, walking over to Kyle. As I drew nearer I saw that he was drunker than I'd thought. His eyes were unfocused and he slurred his words; his breath smelled strongly of alcohol.

"What do you want, Neve?"

I took away his glass of gin and put it firmly on the table. "Careful," I said. "We need to stay sober. More festivities happening. Why aren't you off having fun with the models and starlets – what are you doing all the way over here?"

"You know why..." Kyle shot me a look filled with rage, and I felt my stomach plummet. I really couldn't deal with this right now.

"Kyle, look, I know things are still awkward now, but..."

### Never Land (The Never Knights #2)

"I thought I'd spend the rest of my life with you," Kyle slurred. "But now I haven't only lost that dream, I've lost something else. My best friend. Even when you're with me you don't notice me anymore; you don't care. You only think of him. You want me to move on, to get over you – or do you just want me to get away so you can have more time with loverboy..."

"Kyle," I insisted. "Please, you're drunk. You don't drink – you know that – you can't handle so much liquor on an empty stomach. Especially not on a ship. Do you want to end up the next Natalie Wood? Do you want them to find your body in the Thames?"

Kyle grinned a slow, sloppy, drunken grin. "See, you do care about me. Always have. Always there to pick me up when I fall. That's why I love you, Neve. You take care of me."

"I can't take care of this, Kyle," I pleaded. "I can't take away your pain – as much as I want to. I need you to help me help you. I need you to try, too. So we can get through this together. I'm still your friend..."

Kyle gulped back tears. "You're the girl of my dreams," he said, his voice wavering. "And I've lost you. My girl. My best friend."

"I'm not the girl of your dreams, Kyle," I said. "That girl – she's out there somewhere. I'm sure of it. And she'll love you so much -- and you'll love her, too. You just have to be open to it, Kyle. I'll always be your friend. I'll always be there for you, but you just have to move on..."

My voice trailed off as we reached the table, where Luc and Steve were sitting and waiting for the rest of us.

"Where's Danny?" I took my place next to Steve.

"There he is!" Steve pointed at Danny, who was just entering the room and heading towards us. Danny looked confused, even awkward, as he sat down to dinner with me on one side and Kyle and Luc on the other. Luc at least tried to smile. Kyle, on other hand, was sending daggers straight through him, a look of complete and utter hatred on his face. Dinner was incredibly awkward, and the five of us ate in silence, the only relief the sound of Steve's lame jokes, which he attempted to crack in a pathetic quest to lighten the mood. Kyle was glowering at Danny the whole time, while Luc looked as if he were holding back his emotions. I flushed. Was this always going to be this way from now on? Were the fame, the fortune, all the people wildly applauding us in the audience each night – were they all worth it if it ended like this, in tears?

I didn't have too much time to think about it. As dinner finished and waiters in white jackets served us delectable looking chocolate mousse for dessert, Clarence Blue stood up, banging on a champagne glass with a fork to indicate the beginning of a toast.

"Ladies and gentlemen," he began. A hush fell over the room along with a shiver of anticipation as he spoke. Clarence Blue's words, I knew, could mean millions in profit or utter failure to a whole lot of people in the room. Where he spoke, money followed. Anticipation hung in the air. "It is my great pleasure to have you all here tonight on the Blue Meridian, our newest venture. You like it, don't you?" The crowd murmured in assent. Clarence paused for a moment, taking in his audience's pleasure, savoring his control over them. "Pretty ship, isn't it?"

They applauded even more wildly.

"Good news is it's one of ours. While our larger ships will be doing trans-Atlantic cruises, this little number here will be offering trips all around the Mediterranean in luxury and style. Blue Enterprises plans to extend our hospitality. Having pleased you on land, we now aim to offer you comfort by sea. After all, we're in the entertainment industry, and what could be more entertaining than a cruise among the stars – literal and figurative, of course."

The crowd was overwhelming in its assent. They cheered all the more loudly at the man's words. Clarence beamed with pleasure. "I can't enjoy such a great little boat like this all by myself, can I? I'm proud to announce that this particular line of business will be taken over by one of my brightest employees, if I do say so myself, my son, Daniel."

Kyle's mouth dropped open. "You're Clarence Blue's son?" he looked at Danny with shock in his eyes. But his surprise was nothing compared to Danny's. Danny had gone pale, his bright eyes dark with confusion and disappointment. My stomach plummeted. So, Clarence hadn't even thought to warn, let alone ask, his son that he was making this announcement. He just figured he'd inform Danny of his newfound job at the same time he told everyone else. My heart ached with vicarious anger.

"Figures," Kyle said nastily. "Who could compete with that? Like he isn't perfect enough…"

"Quiet!" Luc said, shutting Kyle up with a firm

look. But I could see that the revelation had shaken Luc, too.

"That's not the only major business decision I intend to announce to you all tonight," Clarence continued. "I want to talk to you all about RRR – the best record label in the business. For years we've partnered with RRR to bring you the best entertainment and the hottest stars, many of whom got their starts in our venues."

I turned around to see Richard Slayton and Cassandra Curry looking at one another, confused.

"Well, how good was that relationship? So close, in fact, that I decided to buy them!" Clarence chortled. "From now on, I'm pleased to announce that RRR will become a subsidiary of Blue Enterprises."

The room was so silent you could hear a pin drop. None of us – least of all Danny – had expected this. Richard Slayton coughed awkwardly, looking decidedly displeased at the news. He peered down at Danny. "Well, erm, congratulations…" he said. "It's not every day a musician buys the company."

"This has nothing to do with me," Danny protested, but Clarence continued on.

"And I am pleased to announce a new president of

RRR. Someone whose finger is always on the pulse of what's new, what's hot, what's trendy, what's in. Someone who keeps me young, always."

*Oh, no...*

"Veronica Taylor, my wife."

If Clarence's first piece of news had stunned the room, his second piece absolutely floored them. Clarence had been known for strange and sometimes whimsical business decisions, but to let an untrained twenty-one year old former supermodel stand at the helm of one of the biggest heavy-hitters in the music industry?

But none of them could be as surprised, as utterly floored, as I was.

If Roni Taylor was running RRR, that meant that I – along with the rest of the Never Knights – was completely and irrevocably screwed.

# Chapter 17

Luc's jaw dropped. His whole face had gone pale – a mixture of shock and anger. He fixed his eyes on Roni, who was sauntering up to the podium, her sweet smile full of deadly venom. I shuddered as I saw his look of utter rage. He looked back to me, then over to Danny, who looked about as horrified as I felt, and then up to Roni.

"Thank you so much to my *darling* husband," Roni was saying, smiling at the crowd and waving like a beauty-pageant queen. I felt sick to my stomach. The sight of that smile – so full of malice, even as she preened and blushed before her husband – made me want to throw up right here on the table. How could she do this? It was one thing to mess with me, to threaten *me*. But to threaten the whole band? Now that Roni had control of RRR, it meant that she could seek revenge on me the only place that it could truly hurt me. She could hit the band. "I am *so* honored at your trust and faith in me."

Luc spluttered furiously. "I don't believe this," he

said aloud. He fumbled with his drink and I realized that he too was tipsy. "Can't you do something about it?" He turned to Danny. "This is ridiculous – fucking ridiculous. What does this woman want – another way to stick it to loverboy, here?"

Danny turned pale. "What did you say?"

"Luc, please..." I reached out a hand, but it was too late.

"Is this how she wants to seduce you, huh?" Luc turned to Danny. "To make all of us her whores? Listen, you mess around wherever you want – but don't drag us all into your sick mess."

"Luc, don't!" I cried. Danny turned toward me in horror, his eyes blazing with anger.

"You *told him*?" All the love, all the light in Danny's had gone. Instead, he was staring at me with savage, powerful rage. "You told him about Roni?"

"It...I was upset..." I whispered back, feeling my cheeks burn. I had been so stupid, confiding in Luc. I'd been angry; I'd been hurt. I'd needed someone to let me cry on his shoulder for a while. But one look at Danny's face told me the damage I'd done. I'd hurt the person I'd loved the most – taken his sordid family secrets, the ones he was almost too ashamed to admit even to himself, and made a mockery of them, aired out his dirty laundry to the public. He looked sick.

"I'm sorry, Danny..." I turned to him, my eyes wide with fear.

Danny inhaled sharply, pressing my hand urgently with a gesture that spelled less love than anger. "Outside, *now*," he said quietly. "We need to talk." He got up and strode from the room, leaving me to follow behind. I'd never seen him like this. Even when we'd argued he'd always been so loving, so kind – so willing to let me in. But now his eyes were cold, dead. He couldn't even look at me. I felt my heart rise in my throat as I ran after him onto the deck.

"How could you *do* that?" Danny turned to me when we were alone at last. "I can't believe you. I trusted you. Not to embarrass me in front of your friends..."

"They're your friends too!"

"Like hell they are!" he spat. "They're just waiting for me to fuck up so they can swoop in and play the noble hero, and win you away from me. Is that what Luc did? Swept you off your feet?"

"What are you talking about?" I reached out to take his hand, but he pushed me away.

"The most embarrassing, shameful secrets of my life – and you just tell everyone!" Danny was shouting. "What else did you tell him? About my mother? About *Peyton*?"

"I've never told anyone about Peyton," I shot back. "I was upset – that night I found you and Roni together..."

"And you what? You stayed behind to talk to me like a rational adult? You asked me what was going on? No – you acted like a girl, like a silly little girl, and ran off without even granting me the dignity of letting me explain. Left me behind with Roni, who I want nothing to do with. Absolutely nothing!"

"I was shocked...I was hurt..." But his words stung. Deep down, I'd always felt that way. Like a little girl. The age difference between me and Danny, the difference in our experiences – everyone else saw me as a young ingénue unworthy of taking Peyton's place. Was he any different?

"I *told* you," he said. "I wasn't interested in her. I never was. Is that what you think of me, Neve? That I'm a cheater? That I'd cheat on you *while you were standing in the next room*? I'm glad you have so much faith in me..."

"It's not like that, Danny..."

"But instead you ran off to one of your other options. One of the guys you keep around just in case you decide I'm not good enough for you."

"They're my friends."

"Friends you tell that I'm going behind my own father's back to bang my stepmother!" he cried. "How stupid do you think I am?" He turned his back on me. "Of all the things announced tonight, all those shocking news, this was the one that hit hardest, Neve. The one about you. All that, I couldn't care less. It's my father's sordid style to shock, but you. I care so much about...everything about you, this cuts to the core." He ran his fingers through his hair and let out a deep breath. "This was a mistake, Neve. I should have known you didn't trust me..."

"But I do!" I cried. But it was too late. Danny had already stormed out of the room, off the ship, and into the London night.

"Danny, wait!" I called out, looking around, panic in my eyes. I couldn't go back into the ballroom – couldn't face my band mates, face RRR, face this world that was crashing down around me. Twenty minutes ago I had my band; I had fame. I had the love of my life. Suddenly I had nothing. Tears began to stream down my face.

"Danny!"

I ran down the gangplank after him, reeling as my feet touched solid ground. I tried to remember where in this dense network of alleyways Danny had parked the Aston Martin, praying I'd reach him before he drove off. "Come back! Please!"

In contrast to the boat, the alleyway was deserted. A homeless guy in a hoodie was slouched in a corner behind some trash cans; other than that, the alley was dark, empty. I shuddered as I looked around for a street light – utterly lost. "Danny!" I called. "Danny – please!"

"Hey!" The homeless guy staggered to his feet, coming towards me. "Hey, you. Neve."

I stopped short in shock. How did he know my name?

He stepped forward into a patch of moonlight and my heart sank. Standing before me, in a filthy hoodie, his eyes bloodshot, his face covered in cuts and bruises that spoke to a week spent on the streets, was Geoff.

"Geoff..." I whispered. All the breath had gone out

of me at once as terror took hold. "What happened to you?"

"You thought you could fuck me over. Cinderella wasn't invited to the ball. But I'm here now. Still got my invitation. To the band mates of the Never Knights. Includes me, doesn't it? Or at least it did. Before Danny Blue took over..."

"Geoff – you're high." I could see the familiar, terrifying glaze in his eyes. "You need to get some sleep – some medical attention, something...we can help you, but you have to commit to wanting to get off the drugs..."

"Just high on life, Neve! You think you can fuck me over? You've ruined my life, you know. Always teasing me, tempting me, showing off that fine ass, just so you can fuck with my head."

Before I could scream, he'd grabbed hold of my wrists, pinning me against the wall. "I should have known you'd try and find a way to get out of it. You can be the perfect little cock-tease, but when push comes to shove you think you can play the princess card and get out scot-free. But I know what you are, Neve. I know what you'd like guys to do to you. Girls as hot as you ask for it all the time."

"How dare you?" Anger took hold of me, and as I

struggled I spat in his face.

He stepped back, laughing with shock. "You want it rough, huh? You want to be feisty? Well, I'll give it to you rough, no doubt about that..."

"Geoff, no..."

He cut me off with his large frame, his lips pressing against mine, shoving me against the wall so hard that I bled. His mouth tasted like filth – unbrushed teeth, slime, and plenty of cheep booze; I felt vomit rise in my throat as I struggled against him, trying to kick and scream and shout at once. I didn't care about the tabloids – the paps. All I cared about was getting out as quickly as possible. How could Geoff sink so low? Back in the days when he was a band member and my friend, I would have felt guilt for not helping him with his drug problems, but now, I felt only fear.

He punched me clear in the face, making me see stars as blood began to scream from my nose. "Don't scream..." Geoff was tearing at my dress, his fingers finding my panties. I was paralyzed with terror, praying for help, praying for deliverance.

Out of the corner of my eye I saw the steel cover of

a trash can. It was a risk – but it was the only chance I got. As he buried his head in my breasts, his sickening mouth leaving agonizing bites on my flesh, I turned my head.

In a single, swift motion I leaped for the cover, grabbing it in both hands and striking him with it, causing him to stumble back. Blood now dripped from his temple. But he was still standing – albeit staggering – and he wrenched the weapon from my hand.

"You're going to wish you hadn't done that..." He grinned, showing yellow teeth. "Because I'm going to make you sorry." He lurched closer. "So very, very sorry."

"Are you?" From behind me, I heard a curt voice – chilling in its anger. "Are you really?"

Relief flooded through me. Standing in the alleyway, a silhouette in the moonlight, was Danny Blue.

# Chapter 18

"I'd let her go if I were you," Danny said, walking to face Geoff, getting straight in my face. "I've just dialed 999 – the police will be here any minute. So either you run – or you wait for the Metropolitan Police to take you into custody."

"You fucking..." Geoff never bothered to finish his sentence. He ran headlong for Danny, tackling him with a furious, brute force, whaling on him – his movements savage, primal, animalistic.

Geoff might have been taller. He might even have been stronger. But he was also high – and his motions were imprecise, clumsy. Danny expertly grabbed hold of Geoff's wrists, flipping him over with a strangely beautiful grace. It was the sort of move I'd expected to see in martial arts films, not here in a seedy London alleyway. But Danny clearly knew what he was doing. He blocked Geoff's punches, responding with a few kicks and blows of his own, before sending Geoff spinning to the floor.

"Haven't we seen enough of you, yet?" Danny shouted as he began to hit Geoff. "Can't you just leave Neve alone?"

He had subdued Geoff, but his anger had not stopped. Geoff was lying on the floor, groaning with pain, but Danny kept kicking.

"Danny, stop!" I shouted. "The police..."

"Fuck the police!" Danny cried, still punching Geoff. "You little coward – you don't deserve to be treated as well as they'll treat you." He landed a kick square on Geoff's chest. Geoff coughed up blood. "You think you can hurt her, do you? You think you can...."

"Danny – no!"

It was only when the first flashbulbs went off that I realized someone else had come. Not the police. The paps. I looked up, blinded by the light, as ten different flash bulbs went off in my face. My heart sank as I looked over at Danny, at the picture that had been taken.

Danny Blue, assaulting a homeless guy in a hoodie. Danny Blue, assaulting a former band member. Whichever way the story played out, it certainly wasn't good.

Geoff may have been high, but his wits were far

from addled. "Help me!" he began to cry, wailing piteously. "He attacked me – out of nowhere..."

I could see the police lights in the distance; I could hear the sirens. My whole body was sick, shattered. My nose was still bleeding profusely. But the police were coming – the police were here – I was safe...but weak from hunger, from being attacked, from all the emotional blows of tonight. I was so so tired.

Those were the last words I could make sense of before everything went black.

When I came to I was lying on a hard, cold bench.

"Y'all right miss?" A cop was sitting next to me, offering me a glass of water. "You had a pretty nasty scare out there...."

"Fine..." I looked around. Where was I? Some sort of office – no, a police station. Metropolitan Police. I shook my head, the world coming into focus. "I mean, not fine, but..."

"We're going to need to take a statement about what happened. Did you see Mr. Blue commit the assault – did he hurt you, too?"

"Me?" My eyes widened with shock. "No – Danny

didn't do anything. He was protecting me..."

Or at least, that was how it had started. But it wasn't what the cameras had caught. It wasn't what the police had seen. They'd seen a furious, out-of-control Danny whaling on an unarmed man. I swallowed hard. Whatever happened to Geoff, the outcome wouldn't be good for Danny.

A door opened, and Geoff staggered out. His face was covered in blood, his nose clearly broken. Danny had clearly taken a toll on him. But not even his black-and-blue bruises could hide the smug look on his face.

"This isn't over," he spat as he passed me by, led by a cop to another room. "I know everything about you, Neve. I know all I need to know."

His words sent shivers down my spine. I looked around in fear – where was Danny? I caught sight of him through a window – he was in one of the interrogation rooms, giving a statement. He too was bleeding, but he looked almost preternaturally calm, collected. Drained.

My heart went out to him. I wanted to rush to him, to thank him, to apologize, to explain. To take him into my arms. I'd hurt him – and he'd repaid me by saving me. Tears fell down my cheeks. I rose to go to him.

But before I could make it to Danny's side, someone

else did. Clarence Blue, apoplectic with rage, strode past me and into the interrogation room, shutting the door behind him. I couldn't hear what they were saying – but I didn't need words. The sight of their two faces – mouths open in shouts and screams, fury on both faces – told me all I needed to know.

"Come on," a voice made me turn around. It was Steve, and he wasn't smiling. "I've been sent to pick you up and take you home."

"Thank God..." I said, hugging Steve tight. But he was stiff, almost awkward.

"We've got to get on a plane in five hours," he said. "Back to California. And, probably, back to obscurity and Luc's basement." He wasn't looking me in the eye. His face was tight with anger. "Probably better this way," he said.

"What do you mean?"

"I mean," Steve said stiffly, "that in the last few hours, I've had to comfort a sobbing Kyle as he threw up over the side of the boat, deal with an utterly heartbroken Luc, watch you fight with Danny on the boat, watch Danny get into a fist-fight with Geoff, and now apparently deal with the fact that RRR is run by your biggest nemesis." He sighed. "You really do know how to create drama, Neve..."

"It's not like that," I insisted.

"You know – I was supportive of you and Danny. I really was. As the one person in this band who apparently *doesn't* want to sleep with you, I just figured you were happy, and that was great. But I don't know what you're playing at, Neve. With Luc – with Kyle. I just want to play my drums and play some music. Not get involved in a fucking soap opera."

"It's not my fault..." I protested.

"Fine," Steve sighed. "Maybe it isn't. I don't know. Maybe if you weren't so friendly with the guys, maybe if you weren't so sexy, they wouldn't have fell for you. I don't know what I'm saying. But they did, and now it's tearing the band apart. Look, Neve, I don't want to fight, okay? I just...I just want to pack my bags, go home, and pray to God whatever beef you have with Danny's stepmom doesn't hurt the rest of us. Remember that whole "no dating in the band thing?" The thing you were so set on? Yeah, well, it was there for a reason."

He turned away from me. "Sorry," he said, after a pause. "That was mean. I mean – Geoff...what he did, it was awful." He squeezed my hand. But I knew that what he said was true. My actions – my relationship with Danny – had done exactly what I hoped it wouldn't do. It had gotten between us and the band.

"I'm sorry, Steve," I said. "All I did was because I cared for the guys, but with Danny…" I gulped back tears. "It's like the floor fell out from me when I first met him."

Steve's expression softened. "Guess it's real then."

"Must be," I said mournfully.

"Come on," Steve said gently. "Let's go." He led me outside and into a cab back to the hotel our band had called home for the past week or so, where I slept like the dead.

The next morning wasn't much better. I woke up to room service knocking at my door at six in the morning – my bags all packed and ready for the taxi to Heathrow.

"Miss..." the maid said. "I've got a letter for you." She handed it to me. "He seemed pretty set that you read it." She handed it to me; I took it with shaking hands.

*Dear Never,*

It was Danny's handwriting. Clipped, clear, and neat. And painfully formal.

*I must apologize for not being at the hotel to see*

*you off. I hope you have recovered from your injuries – and please believe me when I say I could not be more grateful that I was able to be in a position to help you avoid far worse. I am happy to be able to inform you that I have guarantee that the photographs of all of us will not be reaching the press. My father was kind enough to purchase the rights to all photographs from the photographers, and these have summarily been destroyed. Your reputation – and all of ours – is safe.*

*However, I am afraid I have less fortunate news. My father has reminded me of my duty to Blue Enterprises, and of the debt I owe to my family, and of the responsibilities I hold as his son. It is thus with great regret that I must inform you that I can no longer fulfill my duty as the lead guitarist of the Never Knights to the best of my ability...*

I felt tears begin to stream down my face; I felt myself begin to sob – violently, savagely. I could read between the lines – I knew what he wasn't saying. The price Clarence Blue had extracted from his son for getting our names out of the press. Danny's resignation from the band.

The rest of the letter was curt, formal, perfunctory. Nothing about our relationship – nothing about the time we'd shared. Only *I wish you the best in seeking a new guitarist, and have every confidence that he or she will be a far more suitable candidate than I...*

And the one sentence – the only sign of the loving, kind Danny I had known:

*I believe with all my heart that the Never Knights will see its dreams fulfilled – and that you, Neve, will achieve yours.*

*Yours Sincerely,*

*Daniel Blue*

Not only had I lost the man I loved, but I lost one of my band members. And the band. I had never felt so much pain.

The flight back to America was sickeningly awkward. Steve evidently felt bad about his harsh words from the night before, but news of Danny's departure did little to disprove his main point. The band had imploded – and everyone, from Steve to Kyle to Cassandra Curry, who was short with me than usual, seemed to know exactly who to blame.

We sat in silence – me, Kyle, Luc, Steve, and Cassandra. We didn't talk about it – but the shadow of

**Never Land (The Never Knights #2)**

Danny's departure had fallen over us all.

We'd survived a lot together, the band and I. But could we survive this?

# Chapter 19

The next few days didn't improve matters much. We all went home to our respective houses – to watch, to wait. We didn't talk much; it felt as if there was nothing to say. The day we arrived back home Cassandra Curry called to deliver the news we'd all been expecting – due to the restructuring happening at RRR, the Never Knights' American tour had been indefinitely put on hold. "Until we can resolve this through the proper channels," Cassandra had said. It fell to me to pick up the phone and shamefacedly beg the dean of USC to let me re-enroll for the upcoming semester. I'd had my moments of stardom, but now it seemed I'd fallen to earth. I was just another college student, just another normal kid. Nothing special. The band had fallen apart. And I was single – or at least it seemed that way. Danny wasn't returning my calls. His mobile was perpetually off; I tried to call his office, but a rather curt and snooty woman called Marcie intercepted me to inform me that she was his secretary and no, Mr. Blue wasn't in right now, nor could she say when he would be back. After the fifth or six such phone call, I gave up.

So, was this how we broke up? Danny walking off in a huff and never speaking to me again? I wasn't sure whether to be devastated or furious. I knew I had inadvertently betrayed Danny by telling Luc about his relationship with Roni, but his response seemed to me to be beyond out of proportion to what I'd done. He hadn't even tried to forgive me, to talk it out. He'd just quit me – and the band – in one fell swoop.

And I thought I knew why. Peyton would never have done such a thing. Poor, dead, perfect Peyton would never have let Danny down like that. Even if she might have done one day, Danny would never know. She was frozen in time, her flaws varnished by her tragic death. How could I – or anyone else – compare? My thoroughly human screw-ups, the stress of a real relationship – what good were these things when what Danny wanted was his fantasy of the perfect girl. The girl I could never be.

Still, trying to rationalize it didn't make the situation any less devastating. I spent days in bed, going through boxes of tissues, watching old Hollywood movies and crying my eyes out. I didn't want to face anyone. Not Kyle, whose drunken words had still stung me. Not Steve, who still resented the fact that my romantic intrigues had cost him a chance at stardom. And certainly not Luc – although I couldn't say why. Perhaps I was afraid to admit to him that Danny and I had broken up – afraid of what he'd say, of what he'd do...

Not even my mother's cheery voice on the telephone, telling me she was so glad that I'd made it home in time for Christmas and that I simply *had* to come over to try Mrs. Jostens' newest stew dish that very night, could cheer me up. I just wanted to curl up in bed and hide, utterly alone.

"Will you be inviting any special guests over for Christmas dinner?" My mother asked me. "Anyone...who matters?"

"No," I admitted miserably. "Just me. Alone."

"Don't sound so glum, sweetheart," my mom chirped. "You have us."

Yes, I had my family, and I was grateful for that. But I couldn't help feeling that I was returning home in defeat. Roni had won. My band and my relationship – not to mention my friends – were gone. Not even the thought of

### Never Land (The Never Knights #2)

Christmas pudding and my father's famous rendition of "Oh Holy Night" on the electric guitar could make me forget that.

I sighed as I started packing a suitcase. Maybe it would be good to go back home. Less depressing, at least, than this tiny studio apartment, where I still kept finding reminders of Danny. His toothbrush. His spare shirt he'd let me borrow when it got cold. I closed my eyes, placing the shirt against my cheek, remembering the smell of him. Remembering how much I missed him.

A knock came at the door and for a single, fruitless second, I imagined he had come back to me, to tell me he missed me, to tell me he cared...

"Hello, Neve?" It was Luc. "You in there?"

"Yeah...coming!" I opened the door. He was standing before me with an enormous casserole dish.

"Was just about to leave," he said. "Was cleaning out the fridge and I noticed we had a bunch of food left over from last night. Didn't want to throw it out – thought you might want some."

I smiled. "Thanks," I said. It was nice to see his smiling face. Someone who wasn't mad at me – which felt like a rarity right now.

"You get two forks, I'll stick it in the microwave?" Luc grinned at me, warming my heart.

"Is Steve coming?" I asked.

"Actually..." Luc looked uncomfortable. "He already left. Headed back down to Texas to spend the holidays with his grandparents."

"He left?" *And didn't say goodbye?* My heart sank. In the old days, Steve would never have even dreamed of leaving without saying goodbye. But things were different now, it seemed. "So, I guess he's mad at me too, huh."

"He's not mad," said Luc, sitting down next to me on the sofa. "Just tired. It's been a really stressful couple of weeks for all of us. I think he just needed some time on his own."

"Away from the girl who screwed everything up," I said miserably.

"You didn't screw anything up," Luc said. "Believe me. I did – I was stupid to say that stuff about Roni out loud. I was annoyed at Danny and a bit jealous and I wasn't thinking straight. And besides, if anyone should be apologizing it's *her*. That woman's downright crazy – concocting a takeover of RRR just to get at you and

Danny."

"But it's my fault," I said, sniffling. "Just like Geoff
– this whole stuff with Kyle...."

"Kyle's being an idiot," said Luc. "He needs to
grow up and accept things the way they are. It's not your
job to coddle him..."

"I just feel..." It all came flooding out in one big
vale of tears. My voice grew shaky and I started to sob.
"The band – my friends – my boyfriend – it's all gone, Luc.
I don't know what happened. Everything was going so great
– and now...I've lost everything!"

"Hey..." Luc put his arms around me, hugging me
tight. "Listen. You haven't. You *know* you haven't, Neve.
You haven't lost me."

I looked up at him gratefully. His warmth, his
maturity. The way he'd handled all the drama – not by
freaking out and getting drunk, like Kyle had, or by getting
mad at me and blaming me, the way Danny had. He'd been
there for me – put his feelings out there on the table,
respected my decision to stay with Danny, never made me
feel that I'd done anything wrong...Luc was more than just
the handsome boy who had been my best friend. He was a
man now, in every sense of the word. Courageous.

Compassionate. Strong.

And I'd been so stupid – so blind – that I hadn't been able to see it. I'd let myself get wrapped up in Danny, in the drama, in Roni and Peyton and all the problems we had that I'd ignored the beautiful, steadfast guy right next to me.

"I don't want to step in on Danny's turf – I really don't," Luc said. "But I'm here when you need me. As a friend – nothing more."

"Danny doesn't have any turf anymore," I said. "He wants nothing to do with me."

Luc looked at me, a strange expression in his eyes.

"You mean…"

"He stopped answering my calls after that night with Geoff. Wrote me a letter – that's all. Doesn't return my emails, my texts, nothing. We're over, I guess. I just wish he'd told me..."

"That's awful," said Luc, looking genuinely outraged on my behalf. "I mean – he seemed nice, but that's a *dick* move, Neve. You deserve a hell of a lot better than that."

Being so close to him, feeling his warm body

against my own, feeling loyalty, his trust – it overwhelmed me. I wanted this pain deep down inside me to stop – the pain of loss, the heartbreak that was deeper than anything I'd felt before.

"I know I do," I whispered back. And before I knew what I was doing, I was leaning in, kissing him, wrapping my arms around his neck and bringing his lips closer to mine. Releasing all my tension, my anger, my pent-up worry.

There was no more band, no more Danny. No more of other people's rules I had to play by, fear of hurting Kyle, of causing drama, of the paparazzi catching us out. Nothing to stop me from being free, from following the call of my own desires.

His kiss was natural, passionate. His touch wasn't as expert as Danny's – his movements seemed less calculated – but the natural intensity of his desire was more than enough to fill me with longing. The love that shone in his eyes was overwhelming; I wanted to capture that love, to bring it into myself and my own soul.

Soon we were lying on the sofa, breathless, me taking off his top, him taking off mine. I took him in – the chiseled chest, the dark olive skin. He was beautiful – as beautiful as...no, I wouldn't compare them. I couldn't compare them. I had to forget. I had to *forget.* I closed my eyes as Luc lightly took my breasts into his mouth, his tongue tracing the outline of my nipples, making me moan.

He knew what he was doing. He knew exactly how to please me.

"I knew you'd be beautiful," he whispered into my stomach. "I just didn't think you'd be this beautiful."

He pushed me back onto the couch and began fiddling with my jeans, unzipping them, slipping his hands down into my panties, his mouth heading south....

I felt a pang of fear. This was going so quickly. Days before I'd been doing this in London with Danny – now here I was, about to let Luc go down on me. My body ached for release – but my conscious mind stopped me. Whether or not I had to worry about "the band" any longer, I knew this wasn't a good idea. Rushing headlong into sex again was a surefire way to break my heart – and his.

I pulled his head back up towards my breasts. "Let's...take it slow, okay?"

Luc moved his hands back up to my shoulders, laughing slightly. "I've waited six years, Neve," he said. "I think I can manage to wait a little longer, don't you?"

I laughed as I kissed him. There was something so easy about this – so natural. It felt right, it felt simple, in a way that being with Danny never had. Two friends, comfortable with each other, with years of shared experience, shared jokes, shared trust. Luc would never compare me to another girl – Luc would never keep me dangling, waiting to hear those three little words I'd so badly wanted Danny to say. Luc would never... I had to stop comparing him to Danny! But Danny was still on my mind.

"How about you come spend Christmas day with my family?" Luc said, nibbling at my ear. "No pressure. Not like – you know, a thing. Just a nice day with people who care about you. My mom misses you, you know. Wants to make sure you're eating properly."

I thought of Luc's loving, overwhelmingly friendly family. Certainly a far cry from my terrible dinner with Clarence and Veronica.

I smiled. "Sure," I whispered, squeezing his hand. I loved Luc, he was so familiar, so safe. How can I say "no" to him when he was offering me warmth and security?

As he kissed me again, my thoughts drifted to

Danny, and the guitar he had given me. Part of his heart…I was part of his heart – the knight he thought his mother wanted him to be. My heart felt tender, torn and shattered in a million pieces, but somehow I knew I had to be strong for myself and the guys.

"Luc," I said. "I don't want this affecting our friendship either way, but it's too soon for me…"

"Hush," he said taking my hand and kissing the knuckles. "We're not rushing into anything, but just so you know, I'm still here. I won't leave you at your time of need, and I certainly want to be here in good times, too." He folded me into his arms and held me tight, stroking my back until I fell asleep.

# Chapter 20

I never got to spend Christmas Day with Luc. No sooner had I arrived back home to see my mother and father than they enveloped me with hugs and greeted me with a surprise. We were going to get away from California, from the glittering life and the paps and the life I had known in Beverly Hills, and head to my maternal grandmother's ranch in Arizona, passing the time riding horses, helping with farm work, and getting away from everything associated with the Never Knights. I hadn't told my mother or father the whole truth about what had happened in London; nevertheless, they sensed that something was wrong, and while neither of them brought up the subject directly, they were both treating me far more gingerly than I was used to: surprising me with steaming cups of hot chocolate, giving me random and unsolicited hugs in the middle of the day, generally treating me like a child who needed to be petted. I moaned and whined and complained that I was a "big girl" and didn't need such blandishments, but deep down I appreciated the gestures. Right now I wanted to be a little girl again, curled up in my mother's arms, eating enormous forkfuls of spiced rice with my grandmother, forgetting all the stress of the past few weeks. Luc and I had hugged tightly and tacitly agreed not to deal with the consequences of our impromptu make out session until I got back; having a bit of extra time to think things over made me feel a bit better. As devastated as I was about Danny, was I ready to jump into another relationship right away? Would it make me feel better, or would it only delay the inevitable moment when I fell apart? Plus, I could only imagine how Kyle would react when he learned the news. Losing me to Danny was one thing, but losing me to *Luc*, another long-term band-mate, would be worse still. My heart broke for Kyle, and yet I knew that the problem seemed unsolvable. Kyle only wanted one thing, and that was something I could never give him.

***

Spending Christmas morning at the ranch managed to assuage my hurt feelings somewhat. I was far away from everyone now – far from Danny, far from Luc, far from Kyle. I could focus on the shiny presents under the tree and the sweet smell of nutmeg and cinnamon in the air, trying all the while not to think about Danny. He wanted nothing to do with me – I knew that now. Yet as I stared at the presents under the tree, I couldn't help but wonder, but fantasize – *could one of them be from him?* I'd wanted so badly to send him one, to make contact. But I'd known that even if I did send something, that snooty secretary of his was bound to intercept it, as she'd done with the rest of my calls. Danny and I were over – somehow he'd decided my betrayal was too great to forgive.

"Come on," my mother smiled at me. "Open your presents, sweetheart."

A knock sounded at the door.

"I'll get it!" My dad sprang to his feet. "Probably the pizza."

"Pizza?" My grandmother looked shocked. "Who orders pizza on Christmas morning?"

"I do..." My dad looked confused. "Pizza for breakfast – Christmas tradition in the Knight household. Don't worry – I'll still have room for your cooking."

My grandmother muttered her annoyances in

Spanish as my dad left to answer the door.

"Pepperoni or Hawaiian?" My mother turned to me.

But the voices from the hall didn't sound like any pizza delivery I'd heard. My dad's voice was booming – a second voice, quieter, more restrained, engaged in conversation with him. I struggled to make out the voice – and as I closed my eyes, my heart skipped a beat. It was a familiar low voice, a familiar British accent, a voice I'd loved so long and so well. Could it be...

The first thing I saw when he walked into the room was his long black hair, lustrous and shining like a lion's mane. Then he turned to me, and I saw the look on his face, the rapture and the pain, and the love shining out from his bright blue eyes.

"Danny?" I whispered.

"Neve..." His voice was hoarse, almost trembling. "You look...beautiful." He inhaled sharply, looking at once terrified and overjoyed. "Can we go somewhere to talk?"

My grandmother looked him up and down. "Why don't you two go feed the horses?" she said, raising a suspicious eyebrow at the pair of us.

I nodded and led Danny out to the stables, my heart

racing. Had he just come to explain, to break up with me in person? I couldn't deal with any more heartbreak; I couldn't even look at him.

I said nothing as I began filling the troths full of water, trying to avoid Danny's gaze. But before I could say anything he'd grabbed hold of me, pushing me up against the stable walls, kissing me passionately, his mouth hot and vigorous on my own.

"What are you doing?" I pulled away, utterly confused. "I thought we were through?"

"I've screwed up..." Danny was trying to say a hundred things at once, his words vaulting over one another. "I've screwed up, Neve, and I'm so sorry. But one look at you and all I've wanted to do since I saw you is kiss you like that." Tears sprang to his eyes. "I know I don't deserve your forgiveness – I don't deserve anything at all – but I can't stay away, wanting you like this. I have to try."

My mouth fell open. This certainly wasn't what I was expecting. All the pain he'd caused me, all the hurt, all the heartbreak, seemed to well up to the surface.

"You ignored my calls, my texts, my emails...you didn't want to talk to me..."

He grabbed hold of my shoulders, pulling me to

him. "I know," he said. "I'm sorry. As soon as I agreed to quit the Never Knights and take over my duties as President of Blues Enterprises, my correspondence has been filtered. I didn't know you had sent me all those messages. And I had so many demons, so much shit to deal with – at first I was just angry at you for that one night, and that was it. But Roni and my dad...everything piled on top of me at once. It's my Dad." Tears began to roll down the side of his face. "He needed me to take control of the company – urgently."

"Urgently? How urgently..."

"He's sick, Neve." Tears poured down Danny's face. "And he hasn't got much time. And if I don't fight for my rights, and for yours, Roni will have control of everything. I'm working on something now – and I couldn't risk seeing you or you'd get hurt."

"Danny, what are you talking about?"

"She manipulated him! He's signed everything over to her – given her so much power. And now I've got to get it back, before my father signs his whole life over to her, before it's too late. I had to pretend that you and I were through in order to convince Roni I was willing to do what she wanted." He kissed my forehead. "It's the only way.

But when I was hitting Geoff, out there in the alley, it made me realize there was nothing I wouldn't do for you. Seeing him hurt you like that – and I'm no better. I was selfish. I thought you'd wait for me..." He turned away. "I never thought I could care for someone again like this. So completely. You consume me entirely, and I have to take the risk of Roni finding out and everything else to see you here – because I can't not see you, Neve. I'm so sorry I broke your heart." He looked up at me with trembling lips. "Will you let me mend it, Neve?"

Tears were streaming down my face. "How?"

"Move in with me. Here, in California. I've convinced my dad to let me work from America so that I can finish my doctorate – I want you with me, around me, all the time. It's the only way I can keep you safe from Roni, from Geoff, from everyone that wants to hurt us. Roni can't touch me out here. I know it's soon, Neve, but..."

My mind was reeling. My whole heart was breaking and mending in the same moment. I didn't know what I wanted, what I felt.

But my body knew. Silently, wordlessly, I nodded.

He gathered me into his arms.

"But what about the band?" I asked.

His mouth spread into a mischievous smile. "Plan B," he said, grinning. "Roni is out to destroy you, Neve, and everyone around you, including the band. That's how vindictive she is, and I'm sorry I put you in this position. But I'm working on it, and I need your help. If we play our cards right, we'll have our band back and better than ever..."

At that moment, I was so happy, so overjoyed, that Roni and Geoff and all my fears and worries evaporated. All I wanted was to feel Danny in my arms, to be in his arms. All the pain, the breakup, my rebound with Luc, and all my problems with Roni and the band disappeared as I kissed Danny. Danny and I were together, again, promising to commit to one another, stronger than ever before. Together we had the strength, the power, to overcome all the obstacles that stood in our way.

Two hearts. Two souls.

The lion-hearted.

At that moment, I could believe everything. Especially fairy tales coming true, and happily ever afters never ended.

**Never Land (The Never Knights #2)**

If only that was true.

Never, Danny, Kyle, Luc, and Steve's story
continues in Book 3 of the Never Knights Series

*Never Ending (Never Knights Series #3)*

January 2013

**For Exact Release Date, sign up to get the
New Releases and More Email at:**

http://theEDGEbooks.com

Kailin Gow

EXCERPT FROM

# Saving You Saving Me

## By Kailin Gow

*18 year-old aspiring psychiatrist and high school Valedictorian Samantha (Sam) Sullivan falls for a deeply troubled young man named Daggers during a crisis call on her watch, which leads to the unraveling of her perfect world.*

YA-Mature/New Adult

# Prologue

I'm standing here, holding a key; the one Daggers had given me before he left. "It's the key to my heart," he had said, pressing it into my hands. "You have my heart already, you might as well have everything else," he said softly as he kissed away my tears. He pulled me in close to his chest and held me tight. "We've come a long ways, baby. You and I. But we still have some distance to cover, hurdles to jump, if you want to." He laughed his soft gentle Daggers laugh that always sent flutters to my stomach. "I'm a many-layered SOB, a real messed up nut job, who others have given up on, yet you...you continue to peel away the layers." He played with my hair and kissed my forehead. I sighed. My multi-layered Daggers. Each layer more intriguing than the last, each one bringing me closer to the edge of no return.

"I want to peel away those layers," I protested. "I want to know who you are; deep down, if you'll let me."

Daggers closed his eyes for a moment and inhaled sharply. "I know, Sam, and I've been fighting it. If you knew what's really hidden behind all those layers, you'd stay away from me, as far away from me as possible." He opened his eyes to look at me earnestly. "You deserve to know, though. And I'm giving you that chance. With the key…the key to my safe deposit box. But once you know, there's no going back."

For *More of Saving You Saving Me*, get your copy at Amazon.com. Now Available!

Never Land (The Never Knights #2)
EXCERPT FROM

# Loving Summer

## By Kailin Gow

*When I think of my summers spent at Aunt Sookie's Malibu "pad" as she called it, I think about first kisses, first love, and first heartbreak. I think about my friendship with Rachel Donovan and her brothers Nathaniel (Nat) and Drew. I think of all the sunsets, dawns, and first attempts. And then there was this summer, the summer I grew up, in more ways than one, and everyone noticed, especially the boys, especially Nat.* – Summer Jones

# Chapter 1

## Sunsets and First Kisses

### Summer

I'm standing by the baggage claim area, waiting for my three friends to arrive, and wondering a little if maybe I should have made one of those large cards with their names sprawled across that people occasionally hold up. It at least keeps me from wondering what it's going to be like when they arrive. Oh God, I don't think I've been this nervous since… well, forever.

The card is out. I don't have one to write on, and anyway, I sent Rachel my picture. I wonder if she was surprised about how much I've changed. I mean, the last time I saw her, I still had my braces in, and boys didn't give me a second glance. She was always the pretty one, even if she did like to hide it.

It's been so *long* since I saw her. Any of them. It used to be that I'd spend practically every day with Rachel, because Aunt Sookie babysat her and the others, or Rachel's mother would look after me while Aunt Sookie was busy with her acting academy. I guess none of us need that now, but we can still surf the way we used to, or go to the beach, or anything. When we all used to stay over at Aunt Sookie's place on the beach every summer, it used to be great.

It's been three years now though. Maybe it won't be so good. Maybe I won't even know Rachel so much. We've talked on the phone and online, but a friend you spend all summer with is different to one you just talk to now and again, right? I haven't seen any of the Donovans since they moved away to San Francisco. And what about Drew? What about *Nat*? I wonder what he thought about the picture I sent. Did he like it? Did he see that I'm not some little girl anymore?

"Summer?"

There's a Goth girl coming towards me, all purple streaked black hair, ivory skin and dark makeup, in a t-shirt and jeans that go with her hair like someone has streaked purple dye on them. I stare at her for a good couple of seconds before I see her face fully and rush forward to hug her.

"Rachel!"

I shouldn't have worried about what it would be like with her back. Just hugging her, I *know*. I know that we're exactly the friends we always were. Okay, so she's done something freaky with her hair, but she's still Rachel. We have *so* much to catch up on. I step back from her just so that I can look at her, and I can see her doing the same. It's like we're re-learning what we look like, or something.

"Wow," Rachel says. "You've grown taller, and you're in great shape."

"Volleyball," I explain. "*Competitive* volleyball. Mom thought it would be great for me to pick up a team sport, so I went for that one."

"You always were better at doing what your mom wanted than me," Rachel says. She smiles while she says it, but she's told me about a lot of it.

"You still aren't seeing eye to eye with her?" I ask. Maybe I should join the diplomatic core after this.

### Never Land (The Never Knights #2)

"No, Mom's being a bitch." Rachel's expression darkens, which given the way she looks now is a pretty scary sight. "Ever since she caught Dad screwing around, it's been the same." She shakes her head, and the expression passes, just like that. Maybe it's because it's such a great day no one can stay angry for long. "I don't care, though. I'm here with you, the beach, and Aunt Sookie!"

I hug her tightly again. I've missed Rachel so much. She's like the sister I never had. Talking of siblings…

"Where are Drew and Nat?" I ask with a grin. "You didn't abandon them at the San Francisco airport, did you?"

"I wish. They're here somewhere. There. There they are." Rachel waves over at them and I can't help staring. Drew's grown. He must be over six foot now, and he is chiseled and cut with muscles in all the right places, not really concealed by the plain white t-shirt he wears with his tight blue jeans. He's tanned all over, which makes his blue eyes bluer and his black hair almost blue-black. I remember him as scrawny, maybe cute in a kind of way, but nothing like this. He's now a man with a body and a face that's scorching hot. As for Nat, he's even taller, though maybe not as broadly built as his brother these days. He's leaner, more chiseled, too, which makes his high cheekbones stand out along with his full sensual lips. He's wearing a white t-shirt under a blue and white plaid shirt with loose fitting jeans and boots. They suit him. That deep copper hair of his shines in the sunlight. I can't help staring as the two of them get closer. Almost every female at the baggage claim area couldn't help staring, too.

"Could you maybe not stare at my brothers in open mouthed admiration?" Rachel whispers. "It will only make their egos bigger."

For more *Loving Summer*, get your copy at Amazon.com. Now Available!

**Want to Know More about *The Never Knights Series*, Author Insight, Author Appearance, Contests and Giveaways?**

**Join the Kailin Gow's Official Facebook Fan Page at:**

http://www.facebook.com/KailinGowBooks

**Find Out What Other Books Kailin Has at:**

KailinGowBooks.com

**Talk to Kailin Gow, the bestselling author of over 100 distinct books for all ages at:**

KailinGowBooks@aol.com

and

on Twitter at: @kailingow